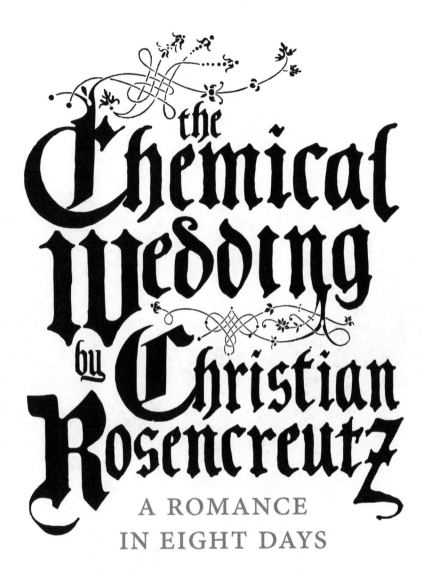

the Chemical Wedding by Christian Rosencreutz

A ROMANCE
IN EIGHT DAYS

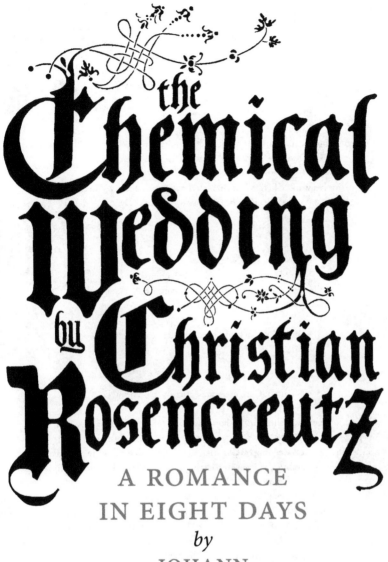

the
Chemical
Wedding
by Christian
Rosencreutz

A ROMANCE
IN EIGHT DAYS

by
JOHANN
VALENTIN ANDREAE

in a new version by

JOHN CROWLEY

illustrated by THEO FADEL

SMALL BEER PRESS · EASTHAMPTON, MASS.

⁊⁊

SMALL BEER PRESS
150 Pleasant Street #306 • Easthampton, MA 01027
smallbeerpress.com • weightlessbooks.com • bookmoonbooks.com
info@smallbeerpress.com

Trade paperback edition distributed by Consortium.

⁊⁊

Library of Congress Cataloging-in-Publication Data

Names: Rosencreutz, Christian, author. | Andreča, Johann Valentin, 1586-1654, author.
| Crowley, John, 1942- author. | Fadel, Theo, illustrator.
Title: The chemical wedding by Christian Rosencreutz : a romance in eight days / by
Johann Valentin Andreae ; in a new version by John Crowley ; Illustrated by Theo Fadel.
Other titles: Chymische Hochzeit. English
Description: Easthampton, Mass. : Small Beer Press, [2016]
Identifiers: LCCN 2015029661 | ISBN 9781618731074 (hardcover)
| ISBN 9781618731081 (trade pbk.) | ISBN 9781618731098 (ebook)
Subjects: LCSH: Society of Rosicrucians.
Classification: LCC BF1623.R7 R6613 2016 | DDC 135/.43--dc23
LC record available at http://lccn.loc.gov/2015029661

⁊⁊

First edition   2 3 4 5 6 7 8 9

Text set in Adobe Garamond Pro.
Printed in the USA.

TABLE OF CONTENTS

Introduction

I

The Chemical Wedding by Christian Rosencreutz is the way I've decided to present the title of this book. Most versions in English are called *The Chemical Wedding of Christian Rosencreutz*, which suggests (and most people who've heard of it suppose) that the wedding is Christian's. It's not; Christian Rosencreutz is the purported *author* of a book called *The Chemical Wedding*. The actual author is Johann Valentin Andreae, whose name didn't appear on the book originally, thus ensuring the confusion. I'll call it herein (as everyone mostly does) simply *The Chemical Wedding*.

Though its original readers would have had a certain amount of context for the truly bizarre and surprising events it tells of, it's possible that *The Chemical Wedding* is now more enjoyable without knowing that context, and experiencing the book unmediated. You might therefore wish to start right in on the first page of text that follows and only then return to this introduction.

Consider a similar case: a little book published in 1934 by the Surrealist artist Max Ernst called *Une Semaine de Bonté*. It was made entirely of collaged illustrations cut out of old books

(Ernst can be said to have invented this now common art medium, actually), and the resulting dream-scenes, seeming to propose a narrative that's actually impossible to discover, are wonderfully mysterious and compelling. You certainly don't need to know that Ernst may have plotted the whole thing according to the principles of ancient alchemy and alchemical practice. In fact, to me at least, knowing that it has such a unifying subtext makes it somehow less interesting, not more.

The Chemical Wedding is also based on or connected to alchemy and alchemical practice, and may even be a parody of such practice, which was taken very seriously when the book appeared. If you have a particular interest in decoding texts along those lines, you may want to investigate those connections; but even if you investigate assiduously, *The Chemical Wedding* will puzzle and may occasionally annoy you with its irreducible strangeness. Read simply as a *story*, however, whatever its meaning, if any, it's perfectly easy to follow and very readable. Sometimes it's very funny. And the allegorical (or symbolic or political or theological) explanations that have been offered can't really account for all that happens in it anyway.

My aim in producing this new version was simply to make this, one of the great outlandish stories in Western literature, accessible to readers in the context of no context. I haven't cut anything or added anything. My biggest contribution was to ask the artist Theo Fadel to take whatever she liked from it and make pictures reflecting her response. Perhaps they'll reflect your own. In addition to this introduction, I've also added some annotations about various historical, literary, and textual matters.

II

The Chemical Wedding by Christian Rosencreutz was published in Germany in 1616, though it probably circulated in manuscript for some time before that. It was presented as the work of a person named Christian Rosencreutz, or Christian of the Rose-Cross, a mysterious magus who died at the age of 106 in 1484 after a lifetime of traveling the world being inducted into the wisdom societies of several lands and forming his own secret society of wise brothers. Ever since, these Brothers of the Rose-Cross have gone about the world healing illness and doing good without our recognizing their presence among us.

That, at any rate, was the story told of him in two pamphlets that appeared, also without any author, just before *The Chemical Wedding* was published. The pamphlets demanded or promised a universal reformation, announced that human knowledge was about to take a vast leap forward, and predicted the fall of many states and kingdoms. These little books, plus *The Chemical Wedding*, which is a very different affair, became the foundation of what has ever after been known as the Rosicrucian phenomenon, or movement, or scare, or hoax. (The Ancient and Mystical Order of the Rose-Cross, or "Rosicrucian Order," is a modern fraternity founded in 1915 and related only in name to the older one.)

Even today it's unclear how these texts came to be, who wrote them, what they intended, and whether there ever was really a mystic brotherhood at all (probably not). It's clear that segments of the society in which they first appeared were very ready to hear what they had to say, insofar as that could be divined, and others felt very threatened by them. Furious debates about religion were under way, in the midst of war and the threat of war between states with different Christian religious establishments; the witch hysteria was intensifying, and there were signs that the world might be coming to an end, or maybe that a new world was about to dawn.

So it was the moment for a craze, and these Rosicrucian challenges and revelations fit the bill. From their manifestos you could deduce that the brothers were able to move among the population invisibly, that they had the means to overthrow the Pope, and that you'd never know who they were or who was allied with them. Of course these ominous possibilities were based on the merest hints and obscure matter in the original documents, which most people didn't have access to, but dozens of later reports appeared, either telling further stories about the original brothers, or begging them to make themselves known, or denouncing the movement as a hoax or a plot. At the right social or historical moment, such manias can spread fast. I had a friend who in the 1950s spent a day fooling around with some pie plates and a camera, tossing the plates into the air and taking grainy pictures of them. It was the height of the UFO mania. He sent the pictures (which he claimed he had snapped by chance) to the local paper and almost instantly they went national. They were making headlines when my friend got cold feet and confessed. His pictures, though, continued to show up in UFO literature for years. It was like that in 1616, I imagine, and the imaginary Rosicrucians have been imbedded in popular mythology ever after.

III

The Chemical Wedding is the only one of the Rosicrucian books whose author eventually came to light. Johann Valentin Andreae was born in Herrenberg, Würtemberg, Germany. His father was a Lutheran pastor, and that's what the son trained to be, though he was apparently not a great student, or didn't care as much for orthodox Lutheran theology as he would later in life; it took him a long time to get a position. His father was very interested in alchemy and did a lot of what we would call lab work in it. After his death Andreae's mother became a court apothecary or pharmacist to a German duke. Paracelsian alchemy, the cutting-edge physical science of the times, was bound up with the beginnings of chemical medicine. So Johann grew up knowing a lot about alchemy, including its downside – his father was always poor because he spent his money on his experiments.

We know that Andreae was the author of *The Chemical Wedding* because he admitted it in a satire written not long after the book appeared, in which he seems to make fun of the whole

Rosicrucian thing, and again in an autobiographical account 25 years later; in that piece he describes *The Chemical Wedding* as a sort of youthful prank – a *ludibrium,* he calls it, a word with more than one shade of meaning: joke, play, nonsense, ridiculous thing. A lot of argument has been occasioned by this word. Committed believers in the deep significance of esoteric texts in general and *The Chemical Wedding* in particular don't want Andreae to scorn or reject his work. Maybe he meant *joke* in the sense of *silly story that masks a deep secret.* Or maybe he meant *play* in the sense of *drama* or *comedy,* which wouldn't imply rejection. On the other hand there are commentators who are sure he dismissed this early work as mere piffle as he grew into a major theologian, thinker, and cleric.

But it seems to me that all Andreae was saying was that *The Chemical Wedding* was never supposed to be taken seriously as a picture of the world, a plan for reform, an alchemical recipe in disguise, or anything like that. And it was just *because* it almost immediately got bound up inextricably with "Rosicrucianism" as a supposed heterodox movement which you could be for or against that Andreae has to pooh-pooh it later. These so-called Rosicrucians were *lying,* he seems to say, but he was *kidding.* His book *was* a hoax, in one sense; in another, it was mental play with the period's hot topics. Above all it was, and ought now to be regarded as, a *novel.* A romance, a fiction, a tale.

More than that: I would contend that *The Chemical Wedding* is not only a fantasy-romance/joke-parody/hoax-tall tale, it is in fact the first science fiction novel.* Such a claim of course has to be based on some sort of definition of "science" (and also "fiction"), but I think it can be sustained. *The Chemical Wedding* predates Kepler's *Somnium* (1634), which usually gets the nod, and *Somnium* (about a dream-trip to the moon) is more of an illustrated example or thought-experiment than a real story; the astronomy underlying it is new, but it doesn't carry the thrill of wild but just-around-the-corner possibilities that SF ought to.

The science that *The Chemical Wedding* builds on is late Renaissance alchemy, which had the same fascination for readers of the time as the scientific possibilities of classic SF did in its last-century heyday: the aliens, spaceships, people-shaped robots, telepathy, time travel. Alchemy is not science if by science we mean only what is now included in that accretion of tested knowledge that still holds up as true even if primitive or inadequate – in this sense Ptolemy's geocentric astronomy is science but judicial astrology is not. Alchemy *is* science, though, in the sense that it had a general picture of the material world and a rational scheme for formulating hypotheses and proceeding with investigations of it. It's also science in the sense that what it attempts to learn about the world will implicitly expand practical human possibilities and powers.

....

* I recently discovered that Everett Bleiler in an essay in *Science Fiction Studies* (2008) argues that *The Chemical Wedding* is a science fiction novel (though not that it's the first) on grounds like mine.

Where it differs from anything we would call science is in the picture of the world it was based on. Alchemy – like astrology, with which it was intimately bound up – supposed that there were common qualities that ran through the universe, able to be discerned alike in plants and animals, stones and metals, planets, and human souls; and though these qualities were physical, they were also moral and spiritual. The universe was shot through with personality: Mercury the metal had the same qualities as Mercury the planet and Mercury the god – it was fast-moving, changeable, tricky, "mercurial." Things, like people, were *jovial* or *martial* or *saturnine* in sharing qualities with Jupiter or Mars or Saturn. In the alchemist's lab, chemical compounds were regarded as persons; they grew angry and hot, they suffered, died, and were reborn, they were transformed from lowly to noble, they could marry and they would procreate. Alchemy didn't work as science, not so much because the alchemists misunderstood the nature of chemical composition and interaction – often they made good observations about that – but because they thought the physical world was pervaded by a psychic and moral order, by *personality*.

Another way in which alchemy differed from modern scientific proceeding was that almost everyone engaged in it was desperate to keep their experiments and their methods secret. Many alchemical works exist telling what the procedures were and what they were supposed to produce, but almost all were written as elaborate allegories, with kings, goddesses, green dragons, red dragons, springs and trees being locked in prison, given wings, murdered, revived, weeping, eaten, etc. It's not always clear what materials are represented by the players in these weird dramas, much less what was actually done with them.

This allegorical masking is further complicated by the general belief that the transformations taking place in the vessels and the furnaces were supposedly also taking place in the soul of the operator, and that only if the operator were "pure" in his intentions and noble in his aims could the Work (as the alchemists called it) succeed.

Given this way of presenting alchemical processes, it might seem that *The Chemical Wedding* is probably an allegory of the Work, with its marriages and its beheaded kings, golden balls in which blue birds are born, white snakes and red fluids, all of them standing not only for physical processes but for the soul-transformation the Work was supposed to effect. In fact the tale has often been interpreted so. But to my mind this doesn't work: Christian, our hero, is not himself the alchemist, only a participant along with others; nor can he be interpreted as standing for any part of the alchemical process. He doesn't understand all that he's seeing, but certainly he is presented as seeing a series of actual events, not an allegory. So far from being transformed or reborn or even made young again, he's actually left at the end worse off than at the beginning, and remains throughout fretful, hopeful, opinionated, and horny – a person, not a symbol. It's not that the transformations and rebirths he *witnesses* don't have symbolic force – they do – but they aren't simply disguises for physical interactions in a furnace, or metaphors for the soul's journey. They are what they are: an account of the farthest-out, most mind-blowing possibilities of a new and unfolding science, witnessed by an Everyman who perhaps doesn't get it all but vouches for its truth. At the same time it's clearly a romance, a flight of fancy, even, yes, a joke.

So that's why *The Chemical Wedding* is the first science fiction novel: unlike other contenders, it's fiction; it's about the possibilities of a science; and it's a novel, a marvelous adventure rather than simply a parable or an allegory or a skit or a thought-experiment. (Like SF, it probably appealed to a self-selected readership of geeks and enthusiasts). Of course Andreae didn't intend it to be taken seriously – after all it's not a theology, not a utopian scheme, not a sermon, all of which he later wrote. But we today think that a fiction – a novel, a story – can be at once unserious and as serious as can be; both a joke and the opposite of a joke; a mirror of nothing and an unforgettable vision. Even science fiction and fantasy, in their different ways, can be those things. Pastor Andreae may have ended up ashamed of it, but we can see it differently.

IV

My version of *The Chemical Wedding* is not a new translation. I have based it on the original English translation by Ezechiel Foxcroft (1690) – he called it "A Hermetick Romance," very justly – and the more modern version, based on Foxcroft, published by A. E. Waite in *The Real History of the Rosicrucians* (1887). I have consulted the recent translation by Joscelyn Godwin (Magnum Opus Hermetic Sourceworks #18, Phanes Press 1991). Andrés Paniagua has given invaluable help, checking my evolving versions against original German printings of the book in European libraries. Still, I make no scholarly claims for this version. I have felt free to expand and contract a bit (though rarely to the extent even of a whole sentence), and I have done things to make the text more readable, such as turning reported or indirect speech into quoted speech and seeking modern equivalents for unfamiliar words and concepts. I have annotated the text for readers who wish for more context, or for explications of various arcana; I make no claim for these notes as being either authoritative or exhaustive. In translating the passages of verse, I chose my own rhyme schemes and meters, and shortened most of them quite a bit. I hope the reader won't mind.

The first thing to be explained about this new version, though, is why I have described *The Chemical Wedding* as "A Romance in Eight Days." The number of days named as such in the text is seven; seven is an important number throughout the book for various groups of persons, collections of items, and actions taken. It's also the number of the planets known to alchemy and astrology, the number of the days of creation, and thus the number of days that the alchemical Work is said to take (Max Ernst's *Un Semaine de Bonté* also takes place in seven days). Certainly the main action of the story does take seven days to complete. But – as the reader will learn who reaches the end of the story – there is an eighth day, a day that is at least as important as the others to the story of Christian Rosencreutz, and – I believe – to the import of the book, though just how it modifies or enlarges that import is a little hard to say.

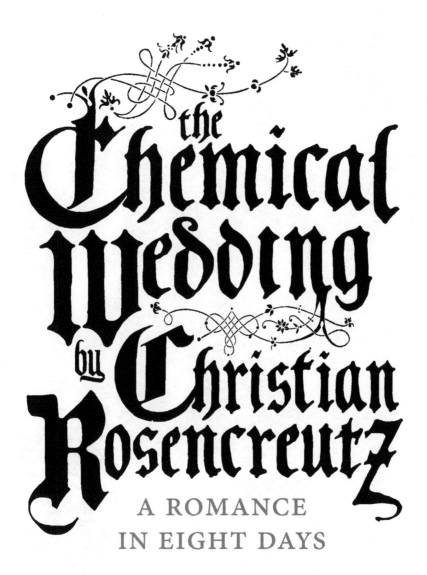

the Chemical Wedding

by Christian Rosencreutz

A ROMANCE
IN EIGHT DAYS

Arcana publicata vilescunt, et gratiam prophanata amittunt. Ergo:
ne Margaritas objice porcis, seu Asino substernere rosas.

❧

Deep mysteries made public are cheapened, and popularized
things lose their value. So don't throw pearls before swine,
or make a bed of roses for a donkey.

The First Book[*]

....

* There are actually no other "books" in the book, though this part title suggests there should be. This is perhaps a setup for the unfinished ending, intended to suggest that further books by Christian would have told more of his story. It emphasizes the weirdly metafictional (not a term the 17th century could have used) character of *CW*.

The First Day

It was just before Easter Sunday,[1] and I was sitting at my
table. I'd said my prayers, talking a long time as usual with
my Maker and thinking about some of the great mysteries
the Father of Lights had revealed to me. Now I was ready to
make and to bake – only in my heart, actually – a small, perfect unleavened wafer to eat with my beloved Paschal Lamb.
All of a sudden a terrible wind blew up, so strong that I
thought the hill my little house was built on would be blown
apart – but I'd seen the Devil do things as bad as this before
(the Devil had often tried to harm me), so I took heart and
went on meditating.

Till I felt somebody touch me on the back.

This frightened me so that I didn't dare turn. I tried to
stay as brave and calm as a human being could under the
circumstances. I felt my coat tugged at, and tugged again,
and at last I looked around. A woman stood there, so bright
and beautiful, in a sky-colored robe – a heavens covered with

....

1 Christian's story begins just before Easter, like Dante's *Divine
Comedy*. It can be seen as an allegory of Christ's death and resurrection, though this idea produces some puzzles.

Till I felt somebody touch me on the back.

stars.[2] She held a trumpet of beaten gold in her hand, and there was a name engraved on it, which I could easily read, but I'm still forbidden to tell it. Under her left arm she had a bundle of letters, in all languages, which she was apparently going to deliver around the world; she had large wings too, full of eyes like a peacock's,[3] that could certainly lift and carry her as fast as an eagle. I might have noticed other things about her too, but she was with me so short a time, and I was so amazed and afraid, that this was all I saw. In fact as soon as I turned around to see her, she started going

....

2 The attributes of this figure – the trumpet, the wings, the letters to the world – identify her as the common allegorical figure Fama, or Fame. A marginal gloss in the original, however, names her in Latin as "Praeconissa" or "Announcer." Throughout the book, Latin marginal glosses signpost the narrative, or explain or decipher (or complicate) various names or symbolic references or codes. The present edition has not included them, but will refer to them here when they seem interesting.

3 Because the spots on a peacock's tail resemble wide-open eyes, the peacock was a common symbol for divine omniscience (seraphim were pictured with peacock wings), but the peacock was of course also a symbol of pride and vainglory. In alchemy the peacock was a symbol of the "rainbow" stage of the chemical process, in which the original matter to be transformed, which has passed through a black or *nigredo* stage, now appears as multi-colored, before passing to the final white (*albedo*) or red (*rubedo*) stage. Those stages were also represented by birds: the crow for the *nigredo,* dove for the *albedo,* etc.

through her letters and pulled one out – a small one – and very gravely she laid it on my table; then, without having said a word, she left. But as she rose into the air, she blew her trumpet so loudly that the whole hill echoed with it, and for a quarter of an hour afterward I couldn't hear myself think.

All this was so unexpected that I had no idea how to explain it to myself, or what to tell myself to do next. So I fell to my knees and begged my Maker not to let anything happen to me that would hurt my chances of heaven. Then, trembling, I went to pick up the little letter – which was heavy, as heavy as though it were solid gold, or heavier. As I was cautiously looking it over, I found a little seal, with an odd sort of cross on it,[4] and

....

4 The marginal illustration here shows not a Christian cross but the alchemical/mystical sign created by the English mathematician and alchemist John Dee, which he called *Monas hieroglyphica,* or "Sacred symbol of the Monad." Dee considered his figure an emblem of the universe and said it included the signs of the zodiac, the Christian cross, the four elements, and other things. It appeared in two books of Dee's that were in circulation in Europe before *CW* appeared, and a version of Dee's explication of it is appended to an earlier Rosicrucian manifesto. Dee himself could be a model for the ideal Rosicrucian: he traveled in many lands, he was a healer, he was humble and

the inscription *In hoc signo vinces*,[5] which made me feel a little better, as such a seal certainly wouldn't have been used by the Devil. I opened the letter very delicately; it was blue inside, and on it in golden letters a poem was written:

On this day, this day, this
The Royal Wedding is!
If you are one who's born to see it,
And if God Himself decree it,
Then you must to the mountain wend
Where three stately temples stand.
From there you'll know
Which way to go.
Be wise, take care,
Wash well, look fair,
Or else the Wedding cannot save you.
Leave right away,
Watch what you weigh –
Too little, and they will not have you!

....

devoted to gaining esoteric knowledge to help others. Frances Yates (*The Rosicrucian Enlightenment*, 1972) suggests that his travels and adventures (which purportedly included summoning angels and making gold) were an inspiration for the Rosicrucian writers.
5 "In this sign [the Cross] you will conquer" – a message supposedly seen, with the image of a cross, by the Emperor Constantine in the sky before a battle. When he won the battle he became a Christian.

Beneath this, images of the bride and groom were drawn – *sponsus* and *sponsa*.

I nearly fainted, having read this; my hair stood on end, and a cold sweat trickled down my side – I was sure that this was the very same Wedding that I had first learned about in a vision seven years before! I'd thought about it often since then, and studied the stars and planets to learn what day it would be, and here it was – and yet I couldn't have known that it would come at such a bad time. I always thought that I'd be an acceptable, even a welcome wedding guest, and I only needed to be ready to go. But now it seemed Providence had a hand in the matter – which I hadn't been certain about before – and the more I thought about myself, the more I found in my head nothing but confusion and blindness about higher things. I couldn't even understand things that lay under my own feet, that I met with and handled every day; much less was I "born to see" the secrets of Nature. I thought that Nature could find a better student almost anywhere to entrust with her precious (though transitory) treasures.

I certainly hadn't been very wise, or taken care, or "washed well" – my health and hygiene, my social life, and my relations with my neighbors, all could use cleaning up. Life was always pushing me on to get more; I was forever wanting to look good in the world's eyes and get ahead instead of working for the good of everyone; plotting how I could make a quick profit by this or that scheme, build a big house, make a name for myself, and all that. But those lines about the "three temples" worried me the most; I couldn't figure out what they meant at all (and I'd still be worrying about it if it hadn't been revealed to me later on).

I was stuck between hope and fear, questioning myself over and over and finding nothing but faults and weaknesses, unable to calm down, still alarmed at the threats in that invitation. So I did what I always do – I went to bed, hoping that my good angel might appear to me in sleep and tell me what to do. And that's just what I learned – for God's glory, my own betterment, and, by the way, a warning to my neighbors.

I'd just fallen asleep when I seemed to be in this dark dungeon, chained there with a lot of others. There was no light at all, and we swarmed like bees over one another, which only made things worse. Even though we couldn't see a thing, we'd hear somebody heave himself over the others when his shackles seemed to be a little lighter, though no one was offering to help him – we had no reason to help anybody get up higher, since we were all in there together.

This seemed to go on and on, each of us cursing the others for being helpless and blind, when we heard trumpets and drums, which gives us some hope; and then the cover of the dungeon was lifted a bit, and a little light came in. We all went for it, but anyone who got up over another would be forced back down under the feet of those also trying to get up. Me too – I pulled up my heavy shackles and got out from under the rest and up onto a stone ledge, which I got hold of I don't know how, and fought off others who tried to get on.

We thought we were all going to get free, but no. A number of gents looked in at us from up above through the hole, just having fun watching us struggling and fighting. When they'd had enough, one old white-haired man called down to us to be quiet, and as soon as we were, he said this (I can still remember it):

If each of you would just desist
From treading underfoot the rest
My mother would, I'm sure, help all;
But since that isn't happening
You'll lie in prison suffering.
Well, never mind: my mother will
Be watching all your madness still,
Displaying in the light up here
Her gifts, which you cannot get near.
But now in honor of the feast,
And that her grace may be increased,
A rope is going to be let down
And all of those who can hang on
Will be pulled out, and so set free.
Who will these lucky persons be?

He hadn't even finished speaking when this very old lady came up behind him. She ordered the rope to be let down into our hole seven times, and whoever could get hold of it and hang on would be pulled up. Oh God the panic that ensued, everyone trying to get hold of the rope and keep others off and only getting in each other's way. After seven minutes, a bell rings and the men above pull up four of us. I couldn't reach the rope at all because I'd climbed up on that ledge, which was over against the dungeon wall, and the rope came down in the middle. The rope was let down again, and a lot of people took hold but couldn't hang on because their chains were too heavy or their hands too tender, but they fought off others who might have done better – in fact several were actually pulled off the rope by others who were unable to hold on themselves – that was how crazy we were in our misery. The saddest cases were those who were so heavy it was impossible they could be lifted up just by their hands on the rope – their hands were practically torn from their arms as they tried to hang on.

So five rope-drops drew up very few people; the pullers above were so quick that as soon as the bell rang, up went the rope, though almost empty. The many who remained, including myself, called on God for mercy and salvation, and apparently he heard me at least,[6] because when the rope came down the sixth time some few took hold of it, and then as it was being pulled up it swung from side to side and reached me. I jumped

....

6 Throughout the story, Christian is always thinking of himself as unfortunate, sinful, the least of the least, and yet he continuously lucks out, is chosen for special favors, and wins through. This attitude is consonant with Andreae's Lutheran Christian theology, and is so constant that one major commenter has interpreted *CW* as a Christian allegory.

and grabbed hold above all the others. So I got out, and I was so overcome with joy I never even noticed a bad cut on my head from a rock, which I got coming out. I joined the others from my rope who were helping to pull up the next rope, the seventh and last, because that's what you did. The straining caused the blood to run down over my clothes, but I didn't care.

When the last haul was done, which brought up the most, the old woman ordered the rope put away. She ordered her aged son to go tell the rest of those below what would happen next. He thought for a while and then called down to them:

> *Now all the rest of you,*
> *Should know that all we do*
> *We have intended to.*
> *Don't think my mother there*
> *With you has not played fair.*
> *But let's be of good cheer!*
> *The time is drawing near*
> *When all shall equal be –*
> *No poor, no rich – you'll see:*
> > *He who now lives large and free*
> > *Will then have work to do, and he*
> > *Who's got a world to bustle in –*
> > *Left with nothing but his skin!*
> *So stop all your complaining!*
> *A short time's now remaining –*
> *Then see what we will do!*

As soon as he was done, the cover of the hole was put on again and locked down; the trumpets and drums started up again, but they weren't loud enough to drown out the screaming and wailing of the prisoners in the dungeon below, which brought tears to my eyes. The old woman and her son sat down on seats that had been set for them, and she wanted to know how many had been got out. When she had the number, and had written it in a little golden-yellow tablet, she asked us all our names and wrote them all down too.

She looked us all over, and I could hear her say to her son, "I'm so sorry for the others left in the dungeon! I wish I dared to let them all out."

"That's the way it has to be, Mother," said the son, "and we shouldn't object. Just think – if everyone on earth was a lord, living the good life, then who would be left to do the serving?"[7]

His mother didn't respond, except to say, "Well, anyway, take the shackles off these ones."

I was one of the last to be freed, and I couldn't help bowing to the old woman and thanking God that, through her, I had got out of that darkness into the daylight. Everyone else, seeing me, did the same thing, which pleased her.

Lastly everyone was given a gold coin for a souvenir and to spend along the way. On one side of these was stamped a ris-

....

7 This assorts a little strangely with the revolutionary tone of the poem just spoken.

ing sun, and on the other, as I remember, the letters D.L.S.[8]
We were told that for God's sake and our neighbors' sakes we
should keep quiet about what had happened to us and what we
were given. Then we were allowed to go. But those shackles had
hurt my ankles so badly that I could hardly shuffle, and the old
woman laughed at me. "Don't take it too hard," she said. "Just
let it remind you to be grateful that you were allowed to come
into the light, even though now you're crippled. Go, and take
care of yourself – do that for me."[9]

Then the trumpets blared again – which startled me so much
that I woke up.

Even when I realized it had all been a dream, it was so grip-
ping that I thought I could still feel the wounds on my ankles.
But wasn't this dream really telling me that I ought to go and
at least attempt to be among those present at this wedding?
Certainly! And so like a little child I gave thanks to Him, and
asked that He keep me always in awe of Him, and fill my heart

....

8 The gloss here interprets the letters on the coin as "Deus lux solis"
(God, the light of the sun) or "Deo laus semper" (Praise always to
God). Like so many things in this book, the ambivalent interpretation
is hardly definitive, as we can't tell who added these marginal glosses –
Christian, who doesn't seem to know what the letters mean? Andreae,
explicating his own story? An unnamed annotator?

9 Everett Bleiler (*Science Fiction Studies,* March 2008) notes that
this narrow escape with an unhealed wound foreshadows what will
become of Christian at the end of the book.

by Christian Rosencreutz 45

every day with wisdom and understanding, and lead me (even though I didn't deserve it) to a happy ending at last.

So I prepared myself for the journey. I put on my white linen coat, fastened with a blood-red ribbon bound crossways over my shoulder. I put four red roses in my hat, so that I would stick out somewhat among the crowd.[10] For food I took bread and salt, as a wise man had once told me to do in cases like this – it had turned out to be the right thing too.[11] But before I left, I got down on my knees in my wedding garment and asked God that if what seemed to be about to happen really did happen, that only good would come of it; and I made a vow, that if anything was revealed to me, I wouldn't use it for my own benefit or power in the world but for the spreading of His name and the service of my neighbor.

And with that vow, I left my little room and set out hopefully and joyfully on the way.

....

10 Christian's outfit here is a model of the heraldic arms of the Andreae family: white with a red cross and four roses in the four divisions. How this fits with the rose-cross symbolism of the earlier texts is impossible to determine, though it's one more piece of (ambiguous) evidence that Andreae had a hand in the earlier documents.

11 Salt is a central ingredient of Paracelsian alchemy – maybe Paracelsus is the "wise man" here referred to.

The Second Day

Pretty soon my path entered the forest, and it seemed to me
that all nature had also been getting dressed for this wedding.
The birds sang so beautifully, the young deer skipped so happily,
that it gladdened my old heart, and I couldn't help singing too:

> *Sweet bird, be glad, and praise your Maker!*
> *Lift your voice, and here's the reason:*
> *God's provided well for you,*
> *Everything in its right season.*
> *Be happy, bird, with all you have.*

> *Are you mad at Him who made you*
> *Just a bird and not a man?*
> *Bird, don't let it cause you sorrow,*
> *Believe it's all part of His plan.*
> *Be happy, bird, as who you are.*

> *How should I argue with my God*
> *I, who crawl 'twixt earth and sky?*
> *As if I had the power to strike*
> *Against the powers set on high!*
> *Be happy, Man, as what you are.*

Angry that you're not a king?
Perhaps the fault lies in your sins.
You think God misses anything?
He knows us now, and what we've been.
Be happy, then, with what you have.

I sang it out from my heart, and the forest echoed, and the hills seemed to repeat the last words. I could see a sort of meadow beyond the forest, where three beautiful tall cedars[1] grew, making a cool shade that looked delightful; even though I hadn't come very far, I was weary with longing and wanted to rest there. As soon as I came close, though, I saw a tablet attached to one tree. This is what was written on it:

Hello, Stranger! If you have heard something about the wedding of the king, this is for you. The bridegroom offers you a choice of four ways, marked by us cedars. All of them will bring you to the court, if you don't get stuck. The first is short but dangerous, leading through rocky uplands you will hardly be able to pass through. The second is longer, and winds around, but it's plain and easy if you use your compass and turn neither right nor left. The third is the true royal highway, running through various delightful scenes and shows of the king's, but this road has been assigned to only one in a thousand. No living man may use the fourth way: it will burn, and

....

1 A marginal gloss here conflates these three cedars with the three temples mentioned in Christian's invitation.

is for spiritual bodies only. So choose which of the three you will go by, and stick to it – because whichever you do choose is the one destined for you by unchangeable Fate, and you can't go back without risking your life. These facts will help you, but watch out! You don't know how much danger you are putting yourself in, and if you know of any tiny fault that puts you on the wrong side of the laws of our king, you ought to go back the way you came right now.

As soon as I read this all my joy vanished. I was singing so loud a minute ago, but now I started to worry. Because of course I could see three of the ways ahead of me and knew that it was my choice which way I went.[2] I thought that if I took the rocky way I'd have a bad fall or get killed, and if I took the long way I'd wander off into byways or be delayed somehow on the great journey. I couldn't hope I was that one among thousands who could take the royal way. I could see the fourth way too, but it was bordered with fiery blasts, and I couldn't even

....

2 Such a choice of ways is common in folk-tales, and so is the fortuitous event that makes a choice for the hero – usually a compassionate act of his own. Andres Paniagua makes a case that the four ways represent the four elements: the craggy one is earth, the second is water (you need a compass lest you be lost at sea), the third is air, and the fourth is fire – it burns and is unsuitable for anyone but spirits. This accords with the scale of nobility of the elements from "lower" to "higher," and with the fact that the impostors and quacks who come to the wedding have taken the first, or "low" road.

The birds sang so beautifully, the young deer skipped so happily,
that it gladdened my old heart, and I couldn't help singing too…

come close to it. So I fretted whether I ought to just turn back, not take any of these ways. I was sure I was unworthy. There was my dream, how I had escaped from the dungeon, but how could I rely on a dream?

I was terribly confused, and because I was so tired and hungry I took out my bread and cut a slice of it. I hadn't noticed a pure white dove sitting on a tree above me, who saw this and came down, very friendly, and I gladly gave her some. I was enjoying her company when a nasty black raven, her enemy, attacked her and, paying no attention to me, tried to steal her bread. The dove could only fly away south, with the raven chasing her. I was so angry and hurt for her that I chased after the raven, and without noticing I ran a good distance down one of the ways the poster described. When I had driven the raven away and saved the dove, I saw what I had done – I had already started off on a path,[3] and now (supposedly) I couldn't go back without great danger.

This was all right in a way, but what was bad was that I had left my bag and my bread at the tree and couldn't go back and get them. In fact as soon as I turned to go that way, a wind blew me back, so strong it nearly knocked me flat – but if I just turned around and went on, nothing stopped me.

....

3 A marginal gloss here says that without thinking Christian took the second way. In a religious allegory – one of the ways of understanding the story – the compass would stand for Orthodoxy (or Prudence, or Faith).

If it was going to be so hard to go back at all, I would just have to face it and go on. I got to my feet and decided I would do everything I could to get to the end of the journey before nightfall. There really were a lot of byways to choose from, but I used my compass as I'd been told to do and didn't budge from the Meridian Line of that road, even when the way was so rugged and impassable that I could hardly find it. I kept thinking about the dove and the raven, but I couldn't figure out what they had meant. At last I could see, on a high hill, an imposing gate. I lit off toward it, though it was a long way from where I was and well off the path, because the sun was already setting behind the hills and there was nowhere else around there I might spend the night. I'd been allowed to blunder along wasting time until at last I saw this gate, but maybe I was meant to reach it.

It turned out to be a truly magnificent royal portal, all carved with figures and symbols, every one of which (I learned later) had a particular meaning. Above all this was a pretty large tablet that said *If you have not been invited, go away!* and other things that later I was told I shouldn't reveal. Just as I stepped in, a person in a cloak of sky-blue came out. I gave him a friendly hello, and he returned the greeting, which was gratifying, but then he immediately demanded my invitation. I was so glad to have remembered to bring it! I certainly might have forgotten it – this person would later tell me that many others had.

He read my letter and not only smiled in satisfaction but bowed low.

by Christian Rosencreutz 55

"Come in, come in, my brother!" he said. "You're certainly a welcome guest to *me*. Please, please tell me your name!"

I was very surprised at this welcome and said that I was a Brother of the Red Rose Cross. Now it was his turn to look surprised, and amazed, and glad.

"My brother," he said then, "do you have anything that you can use to buy a ticket?"[4]

"Not much," I said, "but if you see anything I have that you want, please take it."

He looked me over and at length chose the water bottle I carried. In exchange he gave me a gold token which had nothing on it but the two letters S.C.[5] "When it turns out to be useful to you," he said with feeling, "please remember me."[6]

I asked him how many guests had already got in, and he told me and apparently out of sheer friendliness gave me a sealed letter which he said I should give to the next porter inside. Night had come on while we stood together there, and

....

4 Again in folkloric style, Christian has to pass various gates and give offerings, which he luckily has on him, in order to continue.

5 Glossed as "Sanctitate Constantia" (constant in holiness) or "Sponsus Charus" (beloved spouse) or "Spes, Charitas" (hope, love). Why the labeled objects are often given several possible meanings by the author, who ought to know which one is the right one, is unanswerable.

6 This first guardian is likely the one that in the end, Christian is told he must replace; the gatekeeper's delight in seeing Christian suggests that he knows this, though there seems no way he could.

now suddenly a huge beacon was set on fire on the tops of the gates, the outer and the inner, so that anyone still on the way would hurry to get in.

I could see that the path leading from this gate to the castle gate was bordered by walls and planted with fruit trees. Lanterns were hung on every third tree, and a beautiful young woman, also dressed in sky-blue, was moving down the avenue lighting the candles in the lanterns with a glorious torch. It was so amazingly beautiful to watch that I found it hard to get going; finally, though, I thanked the kind porter and went on. I really wanted to know what the letter said that he had given me, but I had no reason to mistrust him and I went on to the second gate.

Like the first gate, this one was covered with mystic symbols, and had a tablet on it which said *Give and you shall receive.* Right under this gate was a lion, chained up, very large and frightening, who rose up when he saw me and gave a terrifying roar.[7] That woke up the second porter, who was lying asleep on a marble slab there.

....

7 In her book *The Rosicrucian Enlightenment,* Frances Yates presents a highly circumstantial interpretation of *CW* not on theological or occult lines but as a political allegory: a celebration of the marriage of the German prince Frederick, the Elector Palatine, to Elizabeth, daughter of James I of England. The lion was the heraldic animal of both the Palatinate and Britain. Yates conflates the magic castle of *CW* with the Elector's castle at Heidelberg, where all kinds of shows, automata, and pageantry were common.

"Don't be afraid," he said, and he shooed away the lion. With my hand shaking, I gave him the letter the first porter had given me, and when he read it he too regarded me with great respect.

"Welcome, a warm welcome to the man I have waited a long time to see!" he said.

He took out a token too, as the first had, and asked if I had anything to buy it with. I had nothing left but my twist of salt, which he accepted very gratefully. The token he gave me also had only two letters on it, S.M. I was just about to ask him what this and the other token meant when a bell began ringing in the castle.

"Run! Run!" the porter told me, "or else everything you've done so far will be for nothing!" Already the lights above were going out. I ran so fast that I couldn't hear what else he said. The same girl who had lit the lights was now racing behind me putting them out, and I never would have been able to see the way except for the light of the torch she carried. I just barely made it through the last gate – I was right next to her as she went in, and the gate slammed shut behind me so fast that a part of my coat was caught in it – I had to leave the coat behind, because I couldn't get the porter to reopen the gate, not for me and not for the others I could hear outside calling to be let in – because (he said) he had given the keys to the young person, who now went off with them into the court beyond.

So there I was, inside the castle gatehouse, which as I looked around seemed so richly decorated and bejeweled that it simply couldn't be equaled. On either side of the door to the castle was a pillar, and on each stood a figure with an inscription: one was smiling, and his sign said "Congratulations!" and the other, who was sad and hooded, had an inscription that said "Condolences!" All of it was so mysterious and weird that I didn't believe the smartest man on earth could have deciphered it, but one day I myself (God willing) am going to explain it all and tell the world.

Within this gate was a fellow who asked me, again, to give my name, which was written down this time in a little vellum book with other names of those who were to be sent in to the Bridegroom. Here I finally was given the true guest token, which was smaller than the other two but much heavier. On it were only the letters S.P.N. Besides this I was given a new pair of shoes, because the floor of the castle there was polished and shining marble. My old shoes I was to give away to a crowd of poor people who, I now saw, were sitting by the gate very patiently and quietly.[8] I gave away my shoes to an old man, and then two pages brought me into a small room, where I was asked to sit down on a bench. They stuck their torches into two holes in the wall and left.

I was alone. After a time I heard a noise, and what seemed to be a couple of men stumbled into the room and bumped into me, though I couldn't see anyone. I had to put up with their bumping and shoving, since I couldn't see where they were.

....

8 These rather Kafkaesque poor people are never seen again: a truly dreamlike moment.

"Please don't do that," I asked, but then somehow I perceived that actually they were two *barbers,* and so I sat patiently and waited for them to do as they liked. One of them (I still couldn't see anyone) very gently cut the gray hair from the top of my head, though it was left long on my forehead and around my ears.[9] I have to say this weird encounter was very upsetting, because they kept shoving me so hard, and I couldn't see them, and I could only think that God was repaying my idle curiosity by letting me fail at everything.

But now the invisible barbers carefully gathered up all the cut-off hair and carried it away with them. The two pages came back in and laughed at me for being frightened. They had only spoken a few words to me, though, when a little bell rang.

"That's the signal for everyone to assemble," they said. "Let's go!"

I followed the two of them along halls and corridors, through door after door, and up winding stairs, until we came into a great hall. A huge number of invited guests were gathered there, and they were of all sorts – kings, princes, emperors, noblemen, but also many men and women of every class, rich and also poor. I was shocked. What a fool you are, I told myself – you've gone and undertaken this journey, with all its toil and trouble, and look now – you know a lot of these folks very well and have never thought very highly of some of them, to tell the truth, and here they all are, and you with all your

....

9 Christian is given a tonsure, the ancient monastic hairstyle, signifying that he is now a postulant in a religious order.

prayers and your begging just barely got in!

Well, that was the Devil talking, and as best I could I tried to just pay attention to what was going on. People I knew were coming up to say hello.

"Brother Rosencreutz!" said one. "You here too?"

"Yes, yes," I said, "helped to get in by the grace of God."

They all laughed at this, as though it was funny to credit the grace of God with such a trivial thing. We swapped stories about how we'd all got here, and it appeared that most of them had had to take the worst way and clamber over the rocks. We were called to the tables then by trumpets, though we could see no trumpets, and the crowd all hurried to get seats as high up as they thought they deserved, so I ended up at the last seat left in the lower-most table with some fairly seedy characters.[10] The two pages who'd seen to the cutting of my hair came in, and one of them said Grace very beautifully, so well that it made my heart glad. Some of the bigmouths though ignored the two, and winked and made faces and vulgar gestures behind their hats.

Food was brought in, and everyone was served, and plates

....

10 The reference is certainly to Luke 14, 8-11: "When thou art bidden of any man to a wedding, sit not down in the highest room…[G]o and sit down in the lowest room; that when he that bade thee cometh, he may say unto thee, Friend, go up higher … For whosoever exalt-eth himself shall be abased; and he that humbleth himself shall be exalted." Christian, as in other places, follows the Gospel injunction while thinking it's his own timidity or lack of gumption.

and cups came and were taken away, as if each of us had his own waiter, though no one at all could actually be seen. Those comedians around me, liberated by the wine, started bragging and telling tales of their supposed achievements; one had done this wonderful thing, this other one something better, the stupidest and most vulgar talking loudest. Ugh! When I remember the impossible deeds and absurd business I heard them talking about, I just want to vomit. They wouldn't stay in the seats they'd got hold of but went around squeezing in next to the nobler guests and telling lies about deeds that neither Sampson nor Hercules could have done. This fellow's ready to take the world off Atlas's shoulders, that one's going to leash Cerberus and bring him out of Hell. They went on and on, and the great lords were so naive, or the liars were so bold, that they got away with it! Now and then one would get his knuckles rapped with a knife, but they paid no mind, and if one of them did something like filch somebody's gold chain, they'd all try similar tricks. Oh, one of them could see the Ideas of Plato, another could number the atoms of Democritus, and more than one knew the secret of perpetual motion. I suppose some of them were clever enough, but they thought much too highly of themselves. One tried to persuade the rest of us that he could actually see the invisible servants who waited on us, and might have been able to convince us if one of those waiters hadn't smacked him right in his lying muzzle – after which he quieted right down, and others around him went as silent as mice.

Some of the men near me I had respect for. They behaved

themselves and didn't brag. They admitted that the mysteries of Nature were great and they themselves were small, and I was glad of that, but the whole loud mess made me almost regret I'd ever come here. These ill-bred braggarts crowding the high table when I was seated so low made me squirm, what with one of those same so-and-so's mocking me for a fool right in my face. The thing is, I had no idea then that there was a further gate to go through; I thought this was the wedding itself, and that it would go on like this, this humiliation that I didn't think I deserved at all. The Bridegroom or the Bride should have invited some other fool than me! Well, that's what this bad world can do to simple hearts – though it did occur to me that, really, this harassment was just a part of that "lameness" that I'd experienced in that dream the night before. But as the uproar went on, this thought only made me feel worse, because there were plenty of people here boasting about *their* supposed visions and trying to make us believe *their* lying dreams.

A soft-spoken gentleman was seated next to me, and I over-heard him talking intelligently about many matters. Now he turned to me.

"What do you think, brother?" he said. "If someone were to come teach those blockheads how to behave, would he be listened to?"

"Certainly not," I said.

"The world's determined to be cheated," he said, "and can't lis-ten to those who want to help. Look at that boaster there, those ridiculous diagrams and foolish notions he's trying to win people over with. Or those with the just-invented mysterious-sounding terms. Trust me, the time's coming when their masks will be pulled off, and everybody will see the hucksters[11] behind them. Maybe then what's pooh-poohed now will be respected again."

While he was speaking, the uproar worsened; but then all of a sudden music began, more solemn and moving than any I'd ever heard. Everyone fell silent and waited to see what would happen next. The music was made by a vast consort of what I thought must be many kinds of stringed instruments, and the harmonies so swept me away that I sat unmoving, and no one spoke for half an hour at least – even those who tried to open their mouths got a smack from some unseen source. I wished that even if the musicians remained invisible I could at least see their instruments.

The music ceased like that, and nothing happened for a long moment, until at the doors there came a blast of trumpets and roll of drums, as imposing as if the Roman Emperor were about to appear. The doors opened all by themselves, and the noise of the trumpets grew almost unbearable. Into the hall came thousands of little candles – not people *with* candles but candles marching in by themselves, rank on rank. Then those same two little pages, carrying torches, brought in a lady of angelic beauty, seated on

....

11 These hucksters and deceivers, among whom Andreae would probably count those who in his time called themselves Rosicrucians, and most alchemists as well, are set up as a contrast to the good real alchemy practiced by the young lady and the wise men of the castle.

a high throne, all gilded, that moved itself. It seemed to me this was the same young lady who had lit and then put out the lights along the avenue as I came in. She wasn't dressed in sky-blue now, but in snow-white glittering with gold, a garment so gleaming we could hardly look right at it. The pages were dressed the same, though not so bright. When the throne reached the middle of the hall and she stepped down, all the little candles bowed down to her. We all stood up, and she nodded her head to us; we too made our bows, and she began to speak in the gentlest tone:

> *I'll tell you, sirs, the king I serve*
> *Is very near where you are sitting;*
> *The princess too, the one he'll wed,*
> *In ceremonies truly fitting.*
>
> *They know you're here, they're glad to see*
> *You have arrived from every county,*
> *And wish that each of you may earn*
> *Their most delightful bounty.*
>
> *He'll see to it that every one*
> *Enjoys the feast tomorrow*
> *And hopes your pleasure won't be spoiled*
> *By other people's sorrow.*

At this all the little tapers made a sad sort of nod of their flames, and the lady went on, somewhat more sternly now:

You all remember how you came –
You had no hesitation:
You are the blessed, and have the gifts –
So said your invitation!

But sirs, some others are here now –
Though you might not believe it –
Who were not called to come at all
And surely don't deserve it.

Some who think they should be here
Are wrong about the matter,
And some who KNOW they shouldn't be
Got in with tricks and chatter.

Tomorrow we'll bring out the SCALES,
A piece of wondrous science,
And each of you will take the pan.
We insist on your compliance!

Perhaps you know your nasty faults
Perhaps you've just forgotten:
Be certain that those special scales
Will weigh you, ripe or rotten.

So if you came without a right
I'll give you just this warning:

Don't take our test, just sit and wait
And go away come morning.

The rest of you, if you are sure
You're ready to be weighed up
Go with your page and take your rest –
In the morning you'll be paid up!

"And I hope," she said then to all of us, "that you make a good choice, because it will be very bad to get this wrong."

Then she leapt neatly back up onto her throne, the trumpets began to sound again, which didn't cheer some of us up at all, and the pages and invisible attendants bore her off. The little candles remained though, one for each of us, going with us as we milled around.

It's indescribable how fussed and anxious we were. The majority decided to go for the scales, and if it didn't work out just go away quietly (if they were allowed). But I'd already added up my virtues and was quite convinced of my ignorance and unworthiness, and I'd decided to stay with the remainder in the hall. Better to settle for a good meal and nothing more than to risk being tossed out on my ear. When the little candles had led out those who'd chosen to be weighed (each into his own little chamber, as I later learned), there were nine of us left at the tables. Our little lights didn't desert us, but within an hour one of the two pages came in carrying a big bundle of ropes. Had we made up our minds to stay? he asked us. We said, sadly, that yes we had. So he took ropes and tied our hands and feet firmly to our chairs, and when that was done, he went off, taking our little tapers with him, which left us in the dark.

Some of us immediately saw how helpless we'd let ourselves be made, and the trouble we were in now, and I myself began to weep silently – for though we hadn't been forbidden to speak, our grief and anguish kept us from uttering a word. The ropes themselves were made in such a way that they couldn't be cut or wriggled out of, so there we were. I did get a little comfort from thinking that many of those who'd gone off to rest in comfort wouldn't fare so well or be so pleased tomorrow – and maybe, by this trial we were undergoing, we few might make up for daring to come here in the first place. Anyway, thinking these not very happy thoughts I fell asleep and had a dream.

It wasn't a dream that seemed full of importance or meaning, but I still think it's worth recounting.

I found myself on a high mountain, overlooking a great valley in which a tremendous number of people were gathered. And somehow each of them was hanging from a rope attached to their heads. Some of them hung high up in the air and some of them not so high, some low, some just about standing on the ground. There was a little old man flying around among the ropes that held the people up, and he had a big pair of shears, and he'd now and then cut someone's rope. If that person was hanging close to the earth, he'd have a soft landing; but if it was one hanging high up, he made the earth shake when he hit. The threads or ropes apparently grew longer as you hung by them, and if yours wasn't cut, you'd eventually get closer to the ground. I enjoyed watching all this tumbling, and it felt good to see one who, apparently at his wedding, had got up so high that when the little flying man cut his rope he not only fell himself but carried down some of those around him. If your string had let you down close to the ground, though, when you fell you landed so gently that even those right next to you didn't notice.

I was enjoying this funny dream very much when one of my fellow prisoners bumped me and woke me up, which was annoying; but I explained to my brother on the other side about my dream, and I don't know, maybe he got some pleasure from it. Anyway we talked about it and other things through the night, longing for the day.

The Third Day

As soon as the beautiful day broke, and the round red sun lifted himself above the hills and set out across the sky, my dinner companions got out of their doubtless quite comfortable beds ready for the test they'd chosen to take. They came out into the hall and greeted those of us who'd spent the night there, asking with a grin how we'd slept and so on, and some, seeing how we were tied up, lorded it over us for being cowards, not taking our chances as they were doing. But you could see that some of them were feeling they might have guessed wrong and weren't talking so loudly.

We said we didn't know anything and hoped we'd now be set free, having learned a good lesson by our disgrace, and who knows, maybe you fellows have worse than that coming very soon to *you* – but now everyone was assembled and the trumpets began to sound and the drums rolled as they had the night before. We thought that this was it, and the Bridegroom would at last show himself, but no, it wasn't that, it was yesterday's lady again on her move-by-itself throne, now all in red velvet belted with a white scarf. On her head she wore a wreath of green laurel, which looked wonderful on her. Coming in with her now were not little candles but rows of armed men, two hundred of them maybe, all dressed in red and white as she was.

When she dismounted from her throne, she came right over to us who remained and greeted us.

"You've been decently aware of your shortcomings," she said, "and my lord is aware of that and very pleased by it, and has decided you ought to be given a hand up because of it."

Just then she caught sight of me in my outfit, the white linen and red roses. "Well, well," she said to me. "You of all people,[1] deciding to accept the bondage! Why, I would have thought you would have tried for a better spot." Which made my eyes tear up, I'm afraid.

She ordered us all to be unbound from where we sat and then roped together where we could see the scales and the weighing of the others, "because," she said, "it just might go better for you unhappy ones than for some who for now are still free."

Meantime a pair of huge scales, entirely gilded, was set up in the middle of the hall. On a little table covered with red velvet seven weights[2] were placed: first a pretty large one, then four small ones, then two more very big ones. These weights were unbelievably heavy in proportion to their size. The armored

....

1 How the young lady knows who Christian is, and why she thinks he would have tried for a better spot, is unexplained, just as is the apparent foreknowledge of the gatekeepers of Christian's coming. For one guess, see the last note of these notes.

2 Another mystic seven. In a religious allegory, these would be the seven virtues that in moral philosophy combat the seven deadly sins. We learn below that Pride is the sin against the Fourth Weight.

men were divided into seven bands, one for each weight, and out of each band one of them was chosen to be in charge of that group's weight. The lady leapt back onto her throne, and one of the pages commanded all those who wanted to be weighed to get in line in order by rank and step one by one into the pan.

First in the line was an emperor, and without hesitation he stepped up, acknowledged the lady, and in all his imperial regalia got into the pan. The captain of each weight band hefted his particular weight into the opposite pan, and we all were amazed to see that the emperor outweighed them all – all but the last. So he had to get out. He was so upset and cast down that the lady seemed to feel sorry for him, but he was bound with ropes and handed over to the sixth weight band.

After him came another emperor, who stepped haughtily into the pan. He'd hidden a thick book under his gown,[3] and thought for sure he'd make it, but he couldn't even get past the third weight before he was tossed up and pitched out so roughly that his book slipped out. All the soldiers laughed, and he was tied up and given to the third weight band.

It was the same with some other emperors, who were all made fun of and tied up. Then up steps a little short fellow with a curly brown beard, who was an emperor too, and after making his bow to the lady got into the scales and held out!

....

3 Considering how the writers of bad books will be treated, we can guess this book was a quack treatise on alchemy. But the whole of *CW* is surprisingly suspicious of books.

I thought he probably could have beaten a few more weights. The lady arose and bowed to him, presented him with a red gown, and gave him a branch of laurel – she had a good pile of them by her throne – and then invited him to sit down on the steps there below her.

It would take too long to tell how all the other emperors, kings, and lords fared, but not very many held out, virtuous as some were in many ways. Every one of them who failed was laughed to shame by the weight bands. Then it was the turn of the other gentlemen, and perhaps one or two of these, no more, made it through, whether educated or not. After they were sorted, up came those rascal smoke-sellers and scribbling liars, who were pushed onto the scale with such contempt that, badly as I felt, I couldn't help laughing, and neither could those already held prisoner. Those who failed the test were driven off the scale with whips, and so few of them passed that I'm almost embarrassed to tell you – but in fact there were a few good men discovered among them, who received the velvet robes and wreaths of laurel.

So the examination was done, and the only ones left were us poor coupled hounds standing to one side. One of the weight captains stepped forth.

"Gracious lady," he said. "If it's all right, let these poor fellows, who've already admitted their unworthiness, be put on the scale too. No penalties, just for the fun of it, to see what we might learn."

Well, I felt just terrible at this suggestion, because my only comfort had been that at least I wasn't going to have to undergo that shame and be whipped out of the pan. But our mistress consented, so there was no help for it; we were untied and one after the other set in the scale. Most didn't succeed, but at least they weren't laughed at or beaten and taken in custody, but just ordered over to one side. My companion of the night before held out bravely to the end, and everybody – but especially that captain who'd requested we be weighed – applauded, and the young mistress showed him the same respect she had the others.

Two more went up and went right out, and I was the eighth. As soon as I stepped up trembling, my good companion, now already sitting in his velvet robe, gave me a friendly look, and our mistress smiled a little herself. And I beat the weights! Not only that, the lady ordered the weight band to try to lift me by force, and three men hung on the beam of the scale, but couldn't outweigh me.

"*That's him!*" one of the little pages cried loudly, leaping to his feet.[4]

"Well then, set him free!" the other page said.

Our mistress gave the order and I was freed. After I came to her throne, she gave me the choice of releasing one of the captives of the weight bands. That was easy: I chose the first

....

4 Again, Christian seems to be recognized as the necessary person, the hero, which he only ambiguously turns out to be. But see also the final note to the last line of the book.

emperor, whom I'd pitied from the beginning. He was immediately set free and with all respect seated among us.

There was only one more of us to be examined, and he was quickly outweighed. Meanwhile the lady had noticed the roses I had put into my hatband, and she sent her page to ask me if she could have them, to which of course I said yes.

And with that, the first act ended, at about ten in the morning.

The trumpets sounded again, though we still couldn't see them. The weight bands were to step away with their prisoners, who must await the verdict on them, while the weight captains and we survivors of the ordeal made up a council, with the young lady presiding.

"How," she asked us, "should we deal with the ones who failed the test?"

The first suggestion was that they all be put to death, particularly those who'd forced their way in with no regard for the clearly stated conditions. Others suggested they all ought to be put in prison forever. I didn't like either of those suggestions, and neither did our lady president. Finally, myself, the emperor I had freed, and my companion of last night suggested a plan: all the principal lords should be respectfully ushered out of the castle, and the other gentlemen should be stripped and run out naked, while the rest should be driven out with rods, whips, and dogs. The ones who the day before had foregone the examination would be allowed to depart without any blame. But those braggarts and thieving loudmouths who had behaved themselves so badly at dinner should be harshly punished and even pay with their lives, each according to his deeds. The lady approved of that, and voted with us.

But now, apparently, everyone was to be given another dinner, so the announcement and execution of these judgments was put off till afternoon. Our little senate arose, and our young mistress departed in her usual way. They gave the highest table in the hall to us who'd borne the weights, and that was plenty for us until all this day's business was done, after which we understood that we would be conducted to the royal Bridegroom and his Bride. The prisoners were brought into the hall too, and seated according to rank. We made it clear to them that they'd better behave themselves less badly than they had yesterday, but they didn't seem to need the warning; they were already quite subdued.

And I have to say, not out of any impulse to flatter, that really the high-ranking people among the prisoners knew how to bear themselves in their misfortune.[5] They weren't served very well at this meal, though decently enough; they couldn't see their attendants – but to us, suddenly, they were visible! This made me very happy. Fortune had lifted us up, but we

....

5 *CW* exhibits an ambivalence about hierarchy and rank that seems to be pervasive in the period's literature. On the one hand rank is assumed to be justified and is honored; on the other it is thought to be artificial and not correlated with virtue. Christian's dream of the preceding night is an example, and more will come in the trials that the dream allegorizes.

weren't giving ourselves a lot of credit, and we told those prisoners to be of good cheer, things might not work out too badly for them. Of course they wanted to hear more about that, but we were committed to keeping quiet about our decision, and none of us gave any hints.

We comforted them anyway as best we could, drinking with them to see if wine might make them a bit more cheerful. Our table was covered in red velvet and set with cups of silver and gold, which the others stared at in amazement and chagrin. Before we even sat down, the two pages came in and presented everyone at the high table with the Order of the Golden Fleece (with winged lion rampant)[6] and asked us to wear our badges at table and ever after strive to preserve the honor and reputation of that ancient Order which his Majesty now bestowed upon us. We took these Orders humbly and promised to carry out whatever His Majesty required of us as best we could. The pages also brought a paper that showed what our order of precedence was, and I wouldn't mind telling where I stood, except that it might be interpreted as pride: which is expressly against the fourth weight.

....

6 A real order of chivalry, founded in Bruges in 1430 by Duke Philip III of Burgundy to celebrate his marriage to the Portuguese princess Isabella of Aviz. The Fleece is derived from the legendary golden fleece sought for by Jason. Many European monarchs and nobles were (and still are, Queen Elizabeth II among them) members of this very exclusive club. I don't know why it appears here. (The winged lion will appear again in a page or two.)

Our dinner up at the high table was really excellent, and we asked the pages if it would be all right if we sent some choice bits down to friends and acquaintances below, and they made no objection, so everyone sent a little of this and that down by the waiters, whom they of course couldn't see, so they didn't know from whom it came. I decided then I'd take a plate down myself to one of them, but even before I'd got out of my chair one of the waiters took my elbow.

"Just a friendly word of advice," he murmured. "If one of the pages sees you doing that, the king's going to learn about it, and the king's not going to like it. Now, no one's noticed but me, and I won't tell, but in future you should have more regard for the honor of the Order."

"Oh. Yes. Thank you for the warning," I said in some alarm, and sat back down. For a long time afterward I hardly moved. Pretty soon the drums began to beat, which we were getting very used to, and by now knew that it meant our young mistress was about to enter, so we got ready, and here she comes in on her throne with her usual attendants. One of her two pages preceded her with a tall golden goblet, and the other carried a parchment scroll. Having got down from her high seat with marvelous aplomb, she took the goblet from the page.

"This goblet's from the king," she told us, "who gave it to me himself to bring to you, so pass it around in his honor."

On the lid of the goblet was a little golden figure of Lady Luck, very exquisitely made, holding a red pennant in her hand. Seeing that made me drink a little more cautiously;

I had good reasons to know all about that lady's fickleness. The young lady, I noticed, was wearing the same Golden Fleece with lion as we were, and I thought that perhaps she was president of our chapter.

"Can you tell me, Lady," I asked, "what the name of our Order is?"

"Now's not the time to talk about that, with the business of these prisoners unfinished," she told me.

At that she ordered the prisoners to be blindfolded. They probably thought that what we had suffered before as penance was really nothing compared to the high honors we were now getting, which perhaps gave them hope for themselves. Our mistress took a scroll from her page, and turning to the first group of prisoners, she read out from the first part of it:

"First, you lords and gentlemen here. Confess that you believed much too quickly in false and lying books, and because of them believed you could get into this castle if you wanted to, even though you weren't invited. Maybe it was in order to be seen and made much of here and then to go back home with your reputations increased, but once here you egged one another on to worse things, and so you deserve everything that's coming to you."

They very humbly admitted all that and swore to it. Then she turned to address the rest.

"You lot, however, know very well that you concocted fictions and lies, fooled others and cheated them, and offended the king's dignity. You know what unholy meaningless diagrams you've been making use of in your screeds, not respecting even the Trinity itself but persistently deceiving people all over this land. We see now that you tried the same practices here, to ensnare our invited guests and trick the innocent. By all this it's very clear that you've wallowed in every sin you could name, gluttony, fraud, theft, pride, all expressly against the commands of our king, whom you've mocked even among the common people. Therefore you should admit and confess that you're a gang of cheaters and scoundrels who deserve to be cast out of the company of honest people and severely punished."

Some of the better artisans among the crowd were reluctant to admit to all that, but not only was the young mistress charging them with these capital crimes, but now all the other prisoners were also raging at them and yelling that it was all their fault, that they'd bedazzled and seduced them. So rather than get in worse trouble than they already were, they began to say, Well, all right, we're guilty of those things, but it isn't as bad as it seems. Because those others, the lords and gentlemen, had wanted so badly to get into the castle, and offered a lot of money to anyone who could help – so that's all they'd done, they said, tried to use their skills and their arts to come up with something, and that's how they'd ended up here in this pickle. They didn't deserve any worse treatment than the lords just because those schemes and plans they offered didn't work. "These gentlemen surely had the sense to see that if we knew how to get in, we wouldn't sell the secret to them for a pittance and then climb over the walls ourselves to get in!" Sure, they said, their books of secrets sold well, but a man has to make a living, and this is what they had to sell. All they'd done was to take orders and follow them, as good servants should.

All that pleading did them no good. "His Majesty has decided to punish you all, every one of you, although some more severely than others. It's partly true what you say, and so the lords and gentlemen aren't going to be let off, but you have every reason to prepare yourselves for death, you who pushed yourselves forward, and seduced others too, especially the most ignorant, who had no way to resist you. And you have polluted His Majesty's realm with writings that can be shown to be false and baseless right out of their very own pages."

They began sobbing and crying aloud at that, flinging themselves on their faces before the young mistress, begging to be let off this once, all of which got them nowhere – I was amazed to see how resolute our lady was, when many of us were moved to tears by their plight, even though some of them had given us plenty of trouble and bother in the past. No, she just sent out her page, who soon returned with all the armed men who'd presided at the weights. Each one was told to take a prisoner and march him out into the garden. Somehow each one knew exactly which prisoner to go to. Those of us who had spent the night in our chairs were also invited to go, not tied up, and witness the judgment. So we got up, leaving everything on the table (except the goblet with the figure of Fortuna, which the lady gave to the pages to bring). We all climbed on the throne, which moved away as gently as though riding on air, right out the other door and into a great garden, where we got off.

This garden was not particularly remarkable, though it was appealing the way all the trees were planted in neat rows, and there was also an elaborate fountain carved with striking figures and inscriptions and symbols strange to me then, which if I am spared I will describe in a future book. A wooden scaffold stood there, hung with painted curtains; it had four stories, the first more splendid than the others and curtained with white taffeta, so that we couldn't see who was in there. The second story was uncurtained, and empty, and the two above that were again curtained, in red and blue.[7]

As soon as we reached this structure, our mistress bowed down deeply before it, which filled us with awe, as we could guess that the king and queen were probably inside. All of us did as she did, and then she led us up by a winding stair into the second-story gallery, where she sat and gathered the rest of us in order around her. Near me was that emperor whom I'd released before, and I won't tell how this great man deferred to me, not only here but earlier at the table, because I wouldn't want malicious gossips to go spreading the story. I'm sure it was because he could imagine what it would feel like to be down there among those

....

7 Those who understand *CW* as a direct allegory of the Work of alchemy through its various stages make much of these successive colors, as the *prima materia* in the alchemical vessel goes through some of these colors, though not in this order.

to be judged, and not among the honored, where he was because of me.

All at once there appeared among us that wonderful winged person who, dressed in all the stars, had first brought me my invitation to this castle, and whom I hadn't seen since then! First she gave one piercing blast on that golden trumpet and then, in a very loud voice, pronounced sentence on the prisoners.

"The king our gracious lord wishes with all his heart that every one of you assembled here had, in accordance with your invitations, shown yourselves qualified to attend his nuptials. Divine Providence, however, has decreed otherwise. The king, despite his own feelings of compassion, is not going to protest, and will execute the ancient laws of his kingdom. But so that his clemency can be known around the world, he, in consultation with his council and advisors, has modified the usual sentences.

"So the great lords here he freely dismisses, hoping you won't take it badly that you can't be present at the feast, but urging you to remember that God, whose ways cannot be comprehended, sometimes lays more upon great ones such as you than you can sustain. Don't think less of your honor for having been rejected by our Order; everybody can't do everything. Since the works of fakers and hucksters misled you, the king will soon send to each of you a catalogue of all writings known to be untrue, so you can tell good work from bad in future. Pretty soon too he's going to go through his own library and make of all such writings a nice offering to Vulcan, and he suggests you do the same. Above all you are warned never, ever to try to get in here so thoughtlessly again, in case this excuse about 'seducers' isn't allowed next time. Finally, since the estates of this land are as always in need, he hopes that you'll make an offering of whatever you may have about you in the way of a gold chain, or anything of value, and so go safely home again.

"Now. Those of you who could not outweigh the first, the third, or the fourth weight, you aren't to be let off so easily. The king orders you to be stripped stark naked and be driven out.

"You who were lighter than the second and fifth weights, besides being stripped shall be branded with marks indicating which weight you failed."

So the lady continued; those who were outweighed by the sixth or the seventh weight were dealt with more lightly, and so on, with every combination of weights a person failed getting a particular punishment – it's too long to recount it all here[8] – and those who had chosen of their own accord not to be weighed at all were allowed leave without any blame.

"And finally," she said. "Those confidence men and cheaters who couldn't lift any weight whatever: they are condemned to die, by axe, noose, or drowning, as an example to all others."

With that our mistress broke her wand, and the other lady

....

8 If we could be as sure as some commentators claim to be about which weights represent which virtues, we could sort out who is punished in what way for what. Obviously those who were outweighed by the sixth and seventh weights were let off easily because they'd performed pretty well.

blew her trumpet and they turned to make deep reverence to whoever was behind those curtains.

(Now I can't resist telling the reader something about the number of the prisoners, and what weights they lifted or didn't, because as each one came before us I wrote them down in my notebook. There were seven who lifted one weight; twenty-one people lifted two; thirty-five lifted three, and thirty-five also four; twenty-one again lifted five. Seven people lifted six, but only one made it to the seventh weight and couldn't quite raise it, and he was the one I released. Of course there were many who lifted none, and a very few who outweighed them all. What's amazing is that of those who lifted any weights, none lifted the *same* weights as any other – so that some who lifted three, lifted the third weight, the fourth weight, and the fifth weight, and some lifted the first, the second and the third, and so on. So among all 126 who weighed anything, not one was equal to any other! I'd like to give you all their names, with each man's weight, but I'm not allowed yet; I hope someday to be able to, along with the interpretation of it all.)[9]

....

9 John Warwick Montgomery, whose lengthy commentary *(Cross and Crucible,* vol. II) is devoted to proving that *CW* is a Lutheran religious allegory, provides the following equation showing how this is possible:

$$C^r(n) = \frac{n(n-1)\,(n-2)\,\ldots\,(n-r+1)}{1 \cdot 2 \cdot 3 \ldots r}$$

Now the sentences had all been read, and the greater lords were satisfied with theirs, because with all the severity that had been threatened, they'd hardly dared to hope for such a mild one; so in relief they put up as much in gold chains, money, and other valuables as they were carrying, and solemnly got away. The king's servants had been forbidden to make fun of them as they left, but some fellows just couldn't hold it in, and actually it was funny the way they all packed off without a backward glance. Some called out that that catalogue be sent immediately after them, so they could get right to work on their books as His Majesty had asked. At the door, each was given an *Oblivionis haustus*, or Forget-about-it Drink, so he would afterwards remember nothing about the whole embarrassing business.

Those who had chosen not to be weighed, and were allowed to go in peace because of their good sense, were warned not to come back again so weightless and unprepared; if they were to gain some wisdom in the meantime, though, they (and the others likewise) were welcome back.

Meanwhile others were being stripped bare, but also not all given the same treatment, as some were made to wear little

....

$C^r(n)$ is the total number of different combinations of r elements out of n possible elements. For example: if our elements are *1, 2, 3*, then n=3, and if we are looking for distinct combinations of two elements, then r=2 and $C^2(3)=3$, and the distinct combinations are *1* and *2*, *1* and *3*, and *2* and *3*. In *CW*, n=7, the number of the weights, and r can vary from 1 to 6, depending on the number of weights lifted.

bells, and some were scourged out – there were so many differ-ent ways of doing it I can't recount them all.

Then came the last bunch, and the carrying out of their sentences. The soldiers hanged some of them. Some they beheaded. Some they forced to jump into deep water to drown. Others were done in by other means. It all took a long while. Really, I couldn't help weeping to see it, not so much because these were so severely punished, which certainly they deserved, but just from thinking of human blindness and how we will always, always be meddling and prying into things that since Adam first sinned have been simply closed to us.

The garden, which had been so full of people, was at last nearly empty, and except for the soldiers, not a man was left. We sat in silence for the space of five minutes. Then there came forth a beautiful unicorn, as white as snow, wearing a golden collar engraved with certain letters. He came and knelt down on both his forelegs before the great lion that surmounted the fountain in the middle of the garden, who had stood there so immobile that I'd assumed he was made of stone or brass, but who now lifted the sword he held in his paw and broke it in two. He dropped the two pieces into the fountain, where they seemed to sink away, and then he began to roar, and roared and roared until a white dove fluttered down bearing an olive branch in her bill, which the lion ate. He immediately grew calm, and the unicorn pranced back to where she'd come from.[10]

....

10 In some alchemical texts, these represent successive transformations

Our lady led us down the winding stair from the gallery, and we too bowed toward the curtains. We were told to go to the fountain,[11] and there wash our hands and faces, and just wait there awhile until the king had returned to his hall by a secret passage. Thereafter we were taken back to our hall again with pomp and circumstance, music and conversation.

It was about four in the afternoon by now, and so that we could pass the time pleasantly, our lady assigned to each of us a page, who was not only well-dressed but very knowledgeable, in fact able to talk intelligently on so many topics that we had some reason to be abashed. The pages were ordered to act as our guides and give us each our tour of the castle – though only into designated parts – or otherwise entertain us.

"Good-bye then," she said to us. "I'll see you all again at supper, and after that we'll have the Hanging Up of the Weights. Be patient till tomorrow – in the morning you'll be presented to the king!"

So she departed, and we were left to our own devices. Some went to look at the many fine pictures displayed there, and copy them for themselves, and question their guides about the

....

of mercury in the alchemical Work. It's clear that such terms and figures *allude* to the processes of alchemy, but it's difficult indeed to see how they might be fitted into an allegorical scheme whereby all the events recounted in the book *stand for* those processes.

11 This is a healing fountain, as we will learn in the next Day. Water and washing are central alchemical processes.

…and the unicorn pranced back to where she'd come from.

mysterious symbols in them. Others just wanted to go back to eating and drinking. For myself, I asked my page to guide me (and my good companion) around the castle, a tour I will be forever glad I was able to take. Besides the many wonderful antiquities, I was shown the royal tombs, where I learned more about our past kings than I could have in innumerable books. Nearby, an ever-living phoenix could be seen, a being about which I had once written a little study. (If that one ever catches on, I intend to publish further studies, of the lion, the eagle, the gryphon, the falcon, and similar beings, with illustrations, mottoes, etc.). I'm so sorry that my fellow guests passed up the opportunity to see these things, which by God's grace – the only explanation I can think of – I myself was able to see.

I found my page was wonderfully useful on this tour, for these pages had the knack of leading whomever they were assigned to into just the places they'd most enjoy, and the keys to the places that I'd like to see had been given him before-hand. He invited any others to come along who wished to, but I suppose they thought all the important tombs would be in the churchyard and they could get there later and see what there was to see. Never mind: my companion and I sketched all these monuments and copied the inscriptions, and will gladly share them with all students.

The other thing that my page showed us was the royal library. It was all still complete, before the Reformation that had just been ordered by the king. I'll say less about it because the whole catalogue of it is soon to be published, as promised. Right at the entry stands a huge book[12] the like of which I'd never seen before – in it were shown all the pictures, rooms, portals, all the inscriptions and writings, the riddles and the mysteries, that could be seen in the whole castle. I have promised to lay out many of these, and I will, but now's not the time; I need to grow wiser in the ways of the world first.

In every book in the whole library, there was a portrait of its author. A lot of these books were among those which were going to be burnt, as I understood; and thus even the faces of their authors would be erased from the memory of righteous men.[13]

We were about to set out to explore the treasures here when another page came running up to ours and had an urgent whispered exchange with him. Our page, whose face had gone absolutely white, gave him the keys he carried, and the new page ran off with them up a winding stair. We peppered our page with questions about what had happened.

"The king has forbidden anyone to visit either the royal tombs

....

12 More metafiction: *The Chemical Wedding* contains a castle, in which is kept this huge book; the huge book contains in turn the same castle in every detail, including, no doubt, the book itself that Christian is examining, which must again contain the castle and everything in it, etc.

13 It's impossible to decide how Christian, and thus Andreae, feels about this mass book-burning. Montgomery, Andreae's champion, claims that Andreae was appalled by the Reformation book-burnings. There were few at the time who argued that the books of the other side in the religious conflicts ought to be preserved: destroying them was a duty.

or this library," he said. "Please, I beg you, don't tell anyone I let you into them. It would mean my life. I just swore to that other page that we hadn't gone into either place."[14]

We stood trembling, what with the glories we'd seen and the danger we'd been in, but we kept our mouths shut and nobody apparently asked about it later. We'd spent three whole hours in those two places, and I'm not at all sorry.

It was seven o'clock now, and we'd had nothing to eat, but the sights and marvels we consumed were enough for me – with such spiritual nourishment I could fast for a lifetime. We were shown intricately made waterworks, metalworks, and artisans' studios producing work that would surpass ours even if ours were all rolled into one. All these studios and work-places were built in a vast semicircle, all facing a tall clock[15] of the highest quality set up on a beautiful turret in the center, so that the workers could guide their labors by the movements of the planets cleverly modeled there. This gave me a hint as

....

14 It's impossible to understand this page as a figure in an allegory – what does his breaking of the rules, and Christian's covering for him, stand for? (He's about to do much worse.) But he certainly is a vividly real character in a novel.

15 Clockwork and its possibilities stood at the height of Renaissance and Baroque technology (along with firearms and fortifications), and marvelous clocks with elaborate movements showing planetary motions, phases of the moon, and allegorical or religious or fantastic figures with lifelike movements were the rage. There are more to come.

to why our artists never succeed as they might: but it's none of my business to educate them.

We were ushered into a spacious room, one that others were also visiting, and in the middle of it stood a terrestrial globe some thirty feet in diameter, though half of it (except for a couple of steps) was set down into the floor. The whole globe could easily be turned on its axis by two men, but only a half of it was ever seen above the "horizon." I could tell right away that it had some special function, but I couldn't understand what the small gold circles or rings set on it here and there were for. My page laughed and told me to look closer. I could find my own home-place, with a circle of gold on it, and my companion found his too, and all the others standing there found their countries also marked in the same way.

"Yesterday," our page explained, "Old Atlas,[16] which is what we call the royal astronomer, told the king he had determined by the stars the likely home-places of all those who would later be elected to the Order, and marked them with these gold circles. And when I saw that your town, my friend, was among them, even though you'd dropped out of the weight trials, I told the captain of the guard that he should suggest weighing all of the dropouts – as one at least came from a fortunate place.

....

16 Atlas is the mythological Titan who supports the earth with his strength. All astronomy before Galileo adopted Copernicus's heliocentrism was earth-centered – the movement of the heavens around the earth was its subject and study – so Atlas is a good name for an astronomer.

"And that was the reason, by the way, that I personally was assigned to be your guide."

Well, I thanked him very much, and at that studied my town on the globe more closely, and saw that not only was there a gold ring around my home, but that from it there extended faint golden rays – well, I'm not tooting my own horn in saying it, but there it was. Anyway there was more to be learned from this globe and the places marked on it than I want to reveal. Just think about why it is that not every town on earth produces a philosopher.

Our pages then ushered us all right inside the globe![17] There was a hatch, with the builder's name and three dedications inscribed on it, let into the "ocean" part of the globe, and if you lifted that up, you could go in on a walkway to a circular space inside that could hold four people at a time. You could sit there comfortably, and even if it had been broad daylight – it was actually dark by now – you could see the stars. I think they were all sapphires and garnets, glittering brilliantly, all set out in the constellations and moving just as the heavens do.

....

17 This is the kind of marvelous and just-possible machine that a modern science fiction novel would be furnished with. Star globes – globes that pictured the constellations on the outside of a sphere, as though seen from God's point of view – were common, but this one, giving the illusion of a night sky and moved by mechanisms not described, modeling the apparent movement of the stars, would have seemed way cooler.

I kept saying I wanted never to leave – the page later told our young mistress this, who teased me about it, because by now it was supper-time, and I was so entranced by the globe that I was almost last at the table.

When I could linger there no longer, I hurried to put on my same old gown, which I'd removed before, and went up to the high table. The waiters treated me with so much reverence that I was embarrassed to raise my eyes, and I didn't see that our mistress was getting up at my approach, which I shouldn't have let her do – she saw my confusion and tugged at my gown to bring me to a seat.

There's no reason to describe the music and all the rest of the banquet, because it's actually beyond me, and in any case I've described it all as well as I can before. Briefly: it was all beauty and gratification. We talked about what we'd done that afternoon (though I didn't say a word about the library or the tombs). Then, doubtless a little lit up with the wine, the lady presented us with a problem.[18]

"Gentlemen, I'm having an argument with one of my sisters," she said. "In our apartments here, we have an eagle. We both love him dearly, and each of us wants him to love her best,

....

18 These are less problems in logic than insoluble paradoxes, and posing and debating such paradoxes was as popular then as it is now. Montgomery (II, 374-5) goes to terrific lengths to interpret the various figures in the problems as Christ or Christ-like, even the man torn between the old lady and the maiden.

and we fight about it all the time. So the other day we decided to approach him together, and whomever he was more friendly toward, well, she'd be the one who'd have him. So we did, and I had a laurel branch in one hand, as I often do, but not my sister. When we approached our dear eagle, *he* gave *her* a laurel branch that he had in his beak – but then reached for mine! So now each of us thinks that this proves *she's* the better loved one. Can anyone guess how we are going to resolve this?"

This was an interesting proposal, and we all wanted to hear a good answer. Everyone, however, looked at me and wanted me to start. I had no idea what to say, and all I could think to do was to propose a different question instead.

"Lady," I said, "I think I could answer you, if I could resolve a problem of my own. I have two friends, and both of them are extremely fond of me. They wanted very much to know which of them I was more partial to, and what they decided to do was to rush up unexpectedly to me and see which one of them I embraced first. But one was much slower than the other, and fell behind, and was weeping in disappointment even as I, in ignorance, was hugging the other. Later they told me what their plan had been, and I didn't know how to resolve it, and I can't until I get some good advice myself."

The lady was perplexed by this too and could understand my feelings. "Well, let's get both our questions answered," she said, and turned to the others. But I had already shown them the way to respond.

"Back in my home town," the next said, "a young woman

was recently condemned to death. The judge in the case, feeling sorry for the girl, decreed that if anyone wanted to be her champion, he should come forward. Now, she had two men in love with her. One quickly got ready and went into the lists to defend the girl's honor against all comers. The other came too, but a little late – and so what he did was to present himself as the first fellow's adversary and allow himself to be beaten, so that the maiden would go free.

"So tell me, sirs and lady, which of them should win the girl?"

Our mistress threw up her hands at this and said, "I was hoping to get some advice out of you, but I've only got myself in a snare. Still, I'd like to hear more, if there are more."

"Yes, there are," spoke up a third gentleman. "None of these tales is as strange as the one that happened to me. When I was young I loved an honest girl, and in order to get her into bed, I used the services of an old woman who was able to bring us together. Well, just as we three were together, the girl's brothers rushed in on us and were so furious with me they were going to kill me, but I begged and pleaded, and so did the women, and finally instead of taking my life they forced me to swear to marry the dishonored girl – and in every *other* year, to be husband to the old lady instead. Now tell me: which should I have taken to be my wife for the first year – the old one or the young one?"

We all laughed a lot at this one, and though some of us talked it over in whispers, no one was willing to try answering it.

Then a fourth man spoke up. "Once, in a city I know of,

there was an honorable lady,[19] the wife of a nobleman who loved her, as many did, especially one wealthy young lord who wouldn't stop pressing her to give in to him. So at last she told him, 'All right, if in the middle of winter you can bring me into a warm green garden where roses grow, then you can have what you want, but if you can't, you have to stop this and never pester me again.'

"So the young man agreed, and set out to find someone who could bring this off, and at last in a far country he found a little old man who said yes, he could accomplish that – if the young man would make over to him half his inheritance. The lord agreed to this, and the little old man did exactly as he said he could. On a cold winter day, the young man invited the lady to come to his garden, where she was astonished to find the sun warm, the grass green, and the roses nodding. He reminded her of her promise, and she had no choice but to agree; but she begged him to let her see her husband once more before she surrendered to him, and the young man agreed to that.

....

19 This story is actually taken from the *Decameron* of Boccaccio (Day 10, Story 5) and also appears in Book Four of Boccaccio's *Il Filocopo* [Love's Labor] (1536). Bleiler thinks the entire structure of *CW* is based on Italian models, particularly on Boccaccio's *Amorosa visione* [Amorous Vision] (1342-43), "in which the narrator receives a supernatural summons from a maiden (Virtue) to a fête, sets out, chooses between various ways, reaches a splendid edifice where various maidens symbolize abstractions, and sees remarkable displays and festival vehicles." [Bleiler, 2008]

"She confessed to her husband, in tears, what had happened and what she now had to do. Her husband, seeing how clever she had been in trying to stay faithful to him, sent her back to the garden and to the young man, who had purchased her at so high a price, to fulfill the bargain she'd made. But the young lord, when the lady told him all this, was ashamed to touch the honest wife of so honest a man, and sent her home.

"Now he still owed the little old wizard half his inheritance, but that man, poor as he was, was so moved by what these good people had done that he cancelled the agreement he'd made and returned to his country.

"Now, ladies and gentleman, can we tell which of these people showed the greatest goodness?"

We were entirely silenced by that one, and our mistress wouldn't offer an answer either, but only asked anyone else to contribute.

"Well, I'll be quick," said one. "Who has more enjoyment, a person who can look at what he loves, or the one who only thinks about it?"

"The one who can see it," said our young leader.

"No," I said.

So an argument arose about that, until a sixth man called out, "Gentlemen! I'm looking for a wife. Now I have a choice between a virgin, a woman who's now married to somebody else, and a widow. Make this choice for me and I'll take it from there."

"That's all well and good," said a seventh man, "because you have a choice, but in my case I had none.

"When I was young I was wildly in love[20] with a good and beautiful girl, and she loved me too, but her friends and family prevented our marrying. Eventually she married an honest man who treated her affectionately. When she was in childbirth, though, she suffered so dreadfully and it went so badly that everyone thought she was dead. That very night she was buried with mourning and prayers. Now I had a mad idea: In life I couldn't be with her, but now that she was dead, what difference would it make if I were to see her, embrace her, kiss her? So that night I went with a servant and dug her up. I opened the coffin, and there she lay, as beautiful as ever, and I locked her in my arms. But what's this? I seemed to feel a little motion in her heart! It grew stronger from my own warmth around her, and at last I was sure she was alive! I quietly carried her to my house and warmed her cold body with hot baths infused with rare herbs; then I called for my mother, and with her help the lady's child was born, a healthy son, for whom I got a nurse.

"She lay for two days stunned and unseeing. When she could understand, I explained to her all that had happened. I asked her if she would live now with me, for a time at least, as my own wife. But she couldn't bring herself to do so, because of

....

20 This story is also taken from Boccaccio. Montgomery notes this lift, while still attaching a religious allegory to the tale; other commenters draw a theosophical or alchemical moral. This all seems a bit strained since the story is from another source, outside this romance. I myself would use the technical term *padding*.

how terribly it would grieve her poor husband, who after all had treated her well; but she had to admit that, except for that, she owed as much to me as to him.

"So when a couple of months had passed, I invited her husband to dinner at my house, and during the conversation I found a way to ask him whether, if his dead wife should come back to him, he would want to have her. He said oh yes he would; he wept; he lamented her loss sincerely. So I got up and went and brought out to him his wife and son.

"I told him the whole story and then begged him to release her and permit me to marry her instead. He refused absolutely, and we argued long into the night, until at last he had to admit my right, and gave his wife over to me. Now there was still the matter of his son..."

"What!" our young leader broke in. "I can't believe that you would double that poor man's suffering like that!"

"And what about me?" he said. "I didn't have a stake in this?"

We took up the question, and discussed it a long time, though most of us agreed he was in the right. At last he said, "Well, actually, in the end I gave up any claim I had and returned his wife *and* his son to him. But tell me now, which was greater – my selflessness, or this other man's joy?"

The young mistress was so relieved at this that she ordered a toast, just as though it were for that happy husband and wife.

There were other proposals and parables thrown out after that which were puzzling enough that I can't remember them all, but I remember one man saying that a few years before, he'd known of a doctor who bought a cord of wood that kept him warm all winter long, and then when spring came he sold that same wood again – so he had heat for free.

"That's pretty clever," our young leader said, "but we haven't time for more of this."

"All right," said my friend and companion, "then everyone who doesn't understand one of these riddles should send a note to the one who proposed it, and I'm sure he'll be answered."

We said our grace then and arose from the table satisfied and cheerful rather than bloated – I wish it were the same at all such banquets and festivities. We strolled together a bit around the hall, and our mistress asked us if we'd like to begin now on the wedding celebrations. "Oh yes, let's!" one of us cried, and she made a discreet signal to a page while continuing to chat with us.

By now we were on such familiar terms that I dared to ask her name. She smiled at this sally, but she wasn't offended, and she said: "My name[21] contains fifty-five, but it only has eight

....

21 Occasionally *CW* resembles not a novel but a video game, where you have to solve various puzzles in order to ascend to the next level. This puzzle of the lady's name can be solved in more than one way, but I think Bleiler's is the most elegant: The key is substituting letters for numbers in 123 = ABC order. So if there are nine men present, and the young lady's name contains eight letters, then the seventh letter of her name is 9; therefore we know the seventh letter (the ninth in the alphabet) is I. She says the fifth letter and the seventh letter are equal,

letters. The third letter is one-third of the fifth letter, which if you add it to the sixth letter, will give you a number whose square root is more than the third letter by the amount of the first letter, and is half the fourth. The fifth letter and the seventh are equal, and so are the first and the last; and if you add to their number the number of the second letter, they are the same as the sixth letter, which contains just four more than three times the third. So, sir – what's my name?"

....

so in the range 1 2 3 4 5 6 7 8 we have 1 2 3 4 I 6 I 8. Then, since the third letter is ⅓ of the fifth letter (that is, the third letter's numerical value is ⅓ the numerical value of the fifth letter, I, that is, 9) the third letter's numerical value is 3, or C. Now we have 1 2 C 4 I 6 I 8. The sixth letter is four more than the third tripled (3 x 3 + 4), or 13; the 13th letter of the alphabet is M. "The third letter is one-third of the fifth letter, which if you add it to the sixth letter, will give you a number whose square root is more than the third letter by the amount of the first letter, and is half the fourth": the third letter, C (value 3), plus the sixth, M (value 13), produces 16, whose root (4) is the third (3) plus the first (which then must be one) and is half the value of the fourth letter (which must be 8). This produces A 2 C H I M I A. Andreae, who enjoys ambiguities and misdirection and double solutions to a puzzle (as in the love stories, or the interpretations given for the letters stamped on the gold tokens), has misdirected us with the "hint" that the young lady's name "contains fifty-five," which is irrelevant to the solution but has led several analysts (including, apparently, Leibniz!) to assume an algebraic solution and generate pages of calculations.

by Christian Rosencreutz 105

This was complicated enough, but I didn't quit. "Noble lady, could I have the amount of just one letter?"

"Well," she said. "All right."

"What is the number of the seventh letter?"

"The same as the number of gentlemen there are here."

That was enough for me, and I figured out her name easily, which pleased her; she said that much more would be revealed to us.

A flock of her handmaidens[22] had meantime got themselves ready and now came into the hall in a grand procession with music, with two young men carrying torches before them. One of the young men had a smiling face, pleasant features, well-made; the other looked truculent – whatever he wanted he insisted on getting, I would learn. Of the four maidens that followed them, one came in with eyes lowered, very humble; the second, bashful too; but the third seemed alarmed by what she saw, as though she couldn't bear to be where there was so much fun being had – and that would prove to be so too. The fourth brought in bunches of flowers, to show her kindness and generosity.

After them came in two more, a little more grandly dressed – one in a sky-colored robe spangled with gold stars, the other's green and striped with red and white. They wore light floaty scarves or veils on their heads, which I thought were very pretty.

....

22 These girls and their two young men undoubtedly have a symbolic aspect, but what it is I don't know.

Lastly came one all by herself, with a coronet on her head, and her eyes lifted to heaven. We all thought this must be the bride, but no, we were mistaken – in rank and wealth and position, though, she actually surpassed the bride, and all eyes would turn to her throughout the Wedding. We followed our lady and went and knelt before this person, but she was very humble and offered us her hands, telling us not to be amazed – it was the least she could give us. We should raise our eyes to our Creator instead, and acknowledge his power, and go on as we had begun – use this grace she had granted us to give praise to God and do good to others. She spoke so differently from our lady, who was more worldlywise! Her words went right into me. "And you," she said, speaking directly to me. "You have received more than others. See that you give more in return too!"

Actually though, this sermonizing did seem a little out of place, since we'd seen the girls and heard the music, and expected dancing would be next. But no, it wasn't the time for that. The weights which had been used before were still on the red-draped table where they had been first displayed, and the duchess (as I'd learn the grandest of the ladies was titled) told each of the young girls to pick up one of them. Then she pointed to the last and heaviest of the weights. "You may lift mine," she said to our lady. "And all follow me."

Seeing her easily lift that great weight,[23] our high opinion of

....

23 Obviously the young lady isn't all that physically strong, but the weights themselves signify virtues, and the ability to lift them is a part

ourselves was promptly brought down. It was obvious that our
lady had been too kind to us and none of us was as special as
she had let us think. We followed her into the next chamber,
where she hung up the duchess's weight, and a fine hymn was
sung. There was nothing rich or precious in this room, only
some well-made small prayer-books, which such a room should
always have. The duchess knelt on the prie-dieu there, and
we all knelt around her. Our mistress read a prayer from one
of the books, which we repeated after her, that this wedding
might be to the glory of God and our own benefit.

In the next room, the first of the young girls hung up her
weight, and then on into another and another until all the
proper ceremonies were done. The duchess gave her hand to
each of us again and went away with her handmaidens.

Our lady president stayed on with us awhile. It had been
dark now for two hours, and she didn't want to keep us up –
she was very glad to be with us, I thought, but at last she said
good-night and reluctantly went away. Our pages knew what
to do and conducted each of us to his room and remained with
us there too in another bed, so as to be of service in case we
needed anything. My own room (I can't speak of the others')
was grandly furnished with tapestries and paintings, but I was
most delighted with my page, who was so well-spoken and
knowledgeable in all the arts; he spent another hour talking

....

of character, not muscle. Some of the others lifted heavy weights, but
not effortlessly, as this lady can.

with me, and it was half past three when at last I fell asleep. This was my first night in the castle in a real bed, but a nasty dream I had kept me from peaceful sleep: I dreamed that there was a door I couldn't open, couldn't open, but at last I did. Much of the night was spent in these imaginings, until near daybreak I awoke.

The Fourth Day

I was awake and lying in bed next morning, looking idly at the wonderful images and inscriptions all around my room, when suddenly I heard the sound of trumpets, as if a procession were already underway. My page jumped out of bed as if crazed, looking more dead than alive, and you can imagine how I felt when he cried, "They're already being presented to the king!"

I could only groan in frustration and curse my lazy bones. I got dressed, but my page was quicker than I was and ran out of the chamber to see what was what. He soon came back and gave me the good news that I actually hadn't overslept; all I'd done was miss breakfast: they hadn't wanted to wake an old man who needed his rest. But now I had to get ready to go with him to the lion fountain, where most of the others were gathered.

Such a relief! My spirits recovered, and as soon as I had got into my habit, I followed him to the garden I have already told about. I found that the lion, in place of his sword, now held a rather large plaque. Examining this, I could tell that it had been taken from those ancient monuments I'd seen and put here for some special reason. The inscription on it was fading away, so I should set it down here as it was then, and ask my readers to ponder it:

NOW AFTER HUMANKIND

HAS SUFFERED SO MUCH HARM

HERE I FLOW

HAVING BY GOD'S COUNSEL

AND WITH THE HELP OF ART

BECOME A HEALING BALM.

Drink from me if you can; wash, if you like; trouble my waters if you dare.

Drink, Brethren! Drink and live!

(This inscription[2] is simple to read and understand, and I put it down here because it's easier than the ones to come.)

....

1 Hermes is the presiding deity of alchemy: he is the god of shape-shifting, and of money (the alchemists may have personally scorned the search for mere material gold in the Work, but it was a common preoccupation); he is also identified with mercury the element, the basic stuff of much alchemical practice. (He is also famed for tricks, counterfeits, and lying, the god of thieves.)

2 The string of symbols has been interpreted by Richard Kienast (1926) as a *chronogram*, an encoded date, which he works out as 1378, which is Christian Rosencreutz's birth year as given in the Rosicrucian document called *Confessio* for short.

We all washed there at the fountain, and each of us drank the water from a golden cup. Then we followed our mistress back into the hall, and there we put on new robes, all cloth of gold beautifully embroidered with flowers. Everyone also received a new Order of the Golden Fleece, set with gems, each one the work of a different skilled craftsman. On each order hung a heavy gold medallion, on which was shown the sun and the moon; on the back was engraved *The light of the moon shall be as the light of the sun, but the sun will be seven times brighter than now.*[3] We put our previous orders in a case that one of the waiters took away.

Our young mistress led us out in order to the door, where the musicians waited, all dressed in red velvet belted in white.[4] A door I hadn't noticed before was unlocked, revealing the royal winding stairs, and our mistress, with music playing, led us up *three hundred and sixty-five steps*, with all around us nothing but highly finished workmanship and astonishing artifice – the farther up we went the richer it got, until at the top we came

....

3 The quote is from Isaiah: "Moreover the light of the moon shall be as the light of the sun, and the light of the sun shall be sevenfold, as the light of seven days, in the day that the LORD bindeth up the breach of his people, and healeth the stroke of their wound." (KJV) Wounds and their healing, for the alchemists as for Isaiah, always have physical, spiritual, and temporal aspects. The sun stands for gold in alchemy, the moon for silver.

4 Christian's initial dress was white belted with red.

before a painted arch, where sixty maidens welcomed us, all finely dressed. As soon as they curtsied to us and we returned a bow as best we could, our musicians were sent away – they had to go all the way down again, and the door at the bottom was shut after them. A little bell rang, and in came a beautiful young woman bringing us all crowns of laurel,[5] and branches of laurel for our troop of girls.

Just then a curtain was lifted, and there I could see the king and queen, seated in majesty! If the duchess I'd met the day before hadn't spoken to me with such force, I'd have forgotten myself and compared this astonishing beauty to Heaven itself. Apart from the fact that the whole chamber glittered with gold and gems, the queen's robes were made in such a way – well, I couldn't even look directly at them. I thought I'd seen wonderful things in this place, but this surpassed those things as stars do the earth.

The maidens each took a hand of one of us, and with a deep curtsy presented us to the king. "Your Royal Majesties, most gracious king and queen!" our mistress said. "These gentlemen have ventured here, risking life and limb, to honor you, and Your Majesties have reason to be glad of it, since almost all of them are qualified to help improve your lands and realm, as you will find if you examine each of them carefully. I ask your permission, then, to present them to you, and also ask that

....

5 The laurel bough and laurel wreath signify achievement in arts or in games, awarded in the name of Apollo, god of the sun.

I may now resign my commission. Please question them all about how I have performed my duties, both what I did and what I failed to do."

With that she laid down her laurel branch.

Certainly one or another of us should have spoken up right then and said something, but we just stood there all tongue-tied. At last old Atlas the royal astronomer stepped forward and spoke on the king's behalf: "The king and queen rejoice at your arrival, and want you all to know you have their approval and love. Now, Lady, Their Majesties are quite satisfied with your management, and you will be royally rewarded – but still they wish you to remain in their service, as they know they can rely on you."

So our mistress took up her branch again. And with her at last we stepped away.

This great room we had come into was rectangular, five times wider than it was long. At the western end were the thrones under a high arch; like a portal, and there were not one but *three* of them, the middle one higher than the others. Two people sat in each throne: in the first, a very old king[6] with a gray

....

6 A lot of alchemical imagery contrasts elderly kings or royal persons with young ones who are either born from them, or arise from their ashes, or result when the old ones become young again. The old kings are related to Saturn, the old god of time, whose metal is lead (each of the planetary gods had an associated metal); the transforming of old gray lead to young blond gold is one précis of

...there were no bodyguards at all, only a few of the girls who'd been with us the day before, sitting at each side of the arch.

❧

beard, and his consort, who was young and extraordinarily beautiful; in the third throne, a black-skinned king in middle age, and with him a refined elderly woman, not crowned but veiled. The young king and queen sat in the high middle throne, with laurel wreaths on their heads; and over them was suspended a great golden crown. They actually weren't as attractive as I would have thought they would be, but there it is.[7] Behind them on a curved bench sat a group of old men, none with a sword or weapon of any kind, which surprised me – there were no bodyguards at all, only a few of the girls who'd been with us the day before, sitting at each side of the arch.

Now I really must tell you something. All around the thrones, in and out of that high ornamental crown, flew little Cupid

....

the alchemical Work. Andreae here divides the old king into two and gives them each spouses also related to alchemical symbolism, though it's hard to work out how they do the work that as symbols they ought to do. (The White Queen in much alchemical symbolism is the receptive, female principle, embodied in the *albedo* or white elixir; she or it is Luna, the moon, and has the power to transform ordinary substances into silver, the moon's metal. When united with the Red King or male principle, the sun, the two become one and create or generate or give birth to the Philosopher's Stone.)

7 I have long puzzled over this observation of Christian's. Why are his paradigmatic royal persons not sublimely beautiful, and what is his point in saying so? Maybe only because they are *going to be* sublimely beautiful at the end of the process.

himself![8] Sometimes he'd flit down and sit laughing between the two lovers, teasing them with his little bow – in fact he sometimes pretended to be ready to shoot one of us. He was just so full of fun, he wouldn't let even the little birds alone who flew around in that space, chasing and tormenting them. The girls played their games with him too, and when they managed to catch him, he had a hard time getting away. The little villain provided so much delight and laughter!

A small altar of exquisite workmanship stood in front of the queen on her throne, and on it lay a book bound in black velvet stamped with gold, and a little candle in an ivory candlestick. It was a very small candle, and yet it went on burning and never growing shorter, and if Cupid hadn't mischievously blown on it now and then, you wouldn't have known it to be

....

8 With the appearance of Cupid, the story begins an upward ascent in strangeness that continues to the climactic rebirth of the dead king and queen. Cupid is a key figure in the encoding of alchemical secrets; he is often "our Cupid," meaning not the usual one, and stands for Mercurius/mercury. As presented here, he shares the boy Hermes's qualities of teasing and tricking, and yet also for a kind of childish or blameless sexuality that belongs to the Greek Eros. (Some commenters, like Montgomery and the seventeenth century thinker Robert Fludd, want Cupid to stand not just for physical love but for divine or even Christian love, which seems like a stretch to me.) It is dangerous to underestimate or dismiss him, however, as Christian will learn.

fire. Next to this was a small sphere that showed the movements of the planets, very neatly turning all on their own; a
small chiming watch; and a sort of little glass fountain that
bubbled continuously with blood-red fluid. Lastly there was a
skull or death's head, and inside it a white snake. The snake
was so long that it could slide out an eyehole and wind itself
around the objects on the table, yet the tip of its tail still
remained inside, even after its head went back in through the
other eyehole, so that it never entirely left its skull; but when
Cupid gave it a playful tap, it vanished in a moment completely inside. We were amazed.

Up and down the whole room too were statues or figures that
moved by themselves just as if they were alive, worked by hidden
mechanisms I couldn't possibly explain.[9] And as we were passing out of the hall, there came a wonderful sort of singing, and
I couldn't tell for sure if it was the maidens who stayed behind
who sang, or the figures themselves. By now we had seen and
experienced so much that for the time being we could take in no

....

9 Like the tall clock in the artisans' workshop, and the sphere showing the movements of the planets and the chiming watch in the
previous paragraph, these moving statues are high-tech stuff of the
period. They could be clockwork too, or could be made to move by
wind or water moving through them. Some sang, like these, or at least
made sound. (If these statues' movements included walking, they were
beyond any in existence, though.) Nothing more is made of them or
said about them – just another scientific marvel.

more, and our maidens led us down the stairs the musicians had gone down, and the door was locked carefully behind us.

When we were in our own hall again, one of the girls teased our lady president: "I'm amazed, sister, that you dare walk around so freely among so many men."[10]

"Well, sister," said our president, "the only one I need to be careful of is this one," and she pointed at me.

This hurt. It was obvious to me she was making fun of my age, and in fact I was the oldest man there. She saw that I was abashed, and she whispered to me that, if I behaved myself properly with her, she knew how to deal with that problem of age...

But, well, meantime a light supper was again brought in, and everyone sat with his appointed young girl[11] beside him. Those girls were all very skilled in passing the time with interesting conversation, but what their talk and jokes were about – well, I won't tell tales out of school! Honestly, most of the talk was about the higher arts, and it was clear that, old or young, they

....

10 It seems that Cupid's presence and his projection of sexuality is affecting the company. Certainly Christian throughout is pestered with thoughts of sex and of his own aging, which the young woman is suggesting she has ways of overcoming.

11 The male pages and waiters are replaced now with smart and sexy young women. Alchemy was constantly concerned with the sexual urges and couplings of its substances, translating chemical reactions into the biological and the animate, and seeing incest, copulation, and generation in their processes.

knew what they were talking about. For myself, I couldn't stop thinking about how our lady had said she knew how I could maybe regain my youth, and if so how she'd do that, and it all made me a little blue.

The lady saw this and said to everyone, "I'll bet if this young fellow slept with me tonight, he'd wake up feeling a lot better."

Everyone laughed, of course, and I blushed, though I had to laugh too at my own sad situation. One of those present tried to turn the joke back onto the lady who'd started it, and said, "We all heard it, didn't we, and you ladies too, that our directress has offered to sleep with our brother tonight!"

"I'd be very glad to," she responded, "except I'm afraid of my sisters' jealousy – there'd be no dealing with them if I went and picked the handsomest and best man here without their permission."

"All right, sister dear," said another of the maidens, "we can tell that your high position hasn't made you conceited. So it would it be all right with us if you have him, so long as we're allowed to choose – by lot – among all the brothers here, and see which ones *we'll* get to sleep with."

We didn't respond, because we thought it was certainly just joking, and began talking of other things; but our young leader kept teasing us about it. "Come, gentlemen, what about it? Shall we let Chance decide who sleeps with whom tonight?"

"Well," I said, "if that's the way it is, we certainly aren't going to say no."

We decided to try this out right after dinner, and then

immediately decided that dinner was in fact over, and we all
stood and took the hand of the maiden who'd been assigned
to us, to walk with her.

"No no no," said our mistress. "Not so fast. We have to see
how Fortune is going to match us up."

So we separated again, and the girls began arguing about how
to arrange this, but that was just pretend, because our mistress
quickly proposed a plan[12] they all immediately agreed to. She
had us form ourselves up randomly in a circle. Then, starting
from herself, she would count to the seventh person, and that
person would be assigned the person seven down from him or
her, whether that person was a man or maid. We brothers, at
least, didn't guess that there was a scheme afoot, and agreed to
this, but though we thought we'd mixed ourselves up well with
the girls, they knew very well where to put themselves in. The
lady began to count, and the seventh from herself was a maid,
and the seventh from that maid also a maid – and it went on
in this way until every virgin had been hit and not a single
one of us. So there we stood, all of us poor fellows alone, and

....

12 Each of the nine men makes sure that he has a woman either to his
left or his right. But the women see to it that there are always two of
them together. This leaves only one place where a man stands between
two women. The Young Lady stands opposite him. She counts off and
takes the seventh person to her right or left as her partner, and it's a
girl, and that girl does the same. The result is that girls always end up
with girls. It's easy to make a chart of the circle and count off.

had to put up with being laughed at as well for our gullibility. Anyone who'd seen us all mixed together at the start would have thought it was impossible for *none* of us to get chosen, but it was so, and the game was over, and we could only shake our heads over our mistress's trick. Oh well.

Meanwhile Cupid himself had flown into the hall, but he hadn't time to laugh with us or at us, because he was only bringing a loving cup from Their Majesties for us to drink from, and summoning our mistress to the king, and couldn't stay to play. So we drank and thanked him and watched him fly off with her.

Our company must have been looking a little down in the mouth then, and I don't think the maidens were all that sorry to see it, either, but they did begin a decorous dance and invited us to join – I myself preferred to watch, but the more mercurial among my friends were quick to step in, as if they were career dancing-masters.

After a few dances, the lady came back again. "There's to be a comedy," she said, "put on by the artisans and students of the palace, for the entertainment of the royal couple before they depart. Would you like to see it? If so, Their Majesties would be happy to host you in the House of the Sun."

We thanked her very much for this invitation and asked her to bring to Their Majesties our gratitude for the honor. She went off on this errand and came right back bringing word that we were to go back upstairs to where Their Majesties were waiting in the gallery. We didn't stay there long, as the royal procession was already underway – though without any music at all. In the front was that unnamed regal woman I call the duchess, wearing a small rich coronet, dressed in white satin and carrying nothing but a small crucifix made from a single great pearl – the king and his bride had between them revealed it[13] only that day. After her went the royal maidens, carrying the precious items from the little altar. Then the three kings (the old one, the black one, and the middle-aged one), with the bridegroom among them dressed quite plainly in black satin,[14] in the Italian style. He wore a small black hat with a little pointed black feather, which he very graciously tipped when he saw us, while we bowed to him, and to the others, as we'd been instructed to do.

After the three kings came their queens, two of them dressed richly and colorfully, but the bride in the middle was dressed

....

13 "Aufmachen," which in modern German means to open, to open up, to let out. The 1690 Foxcroft translation has the crucifix "made from a pearl" and "wrought between" the king and queen, i.e. made or produced by them – they either made the crucifix from the pearl themselves or *produced* the pearl, as though they were oysters. Godwin (1991) has the crucifix, or the pearl, "revealed between" the royal pair. My rendering, though it may not be accurate, at least makes sense.

14 The royal pair, unlike the symbolic other kings and queens, are dressed plainly in black, suggesting the *nigredo*, the first stage of the alchemical Work, in which the original material is reduced to a *prima materia* without qualities – it is death, rot, entombment, darkness, nothingness, from which the later stages will arise or be born.

all in plain black like her groom: Cupid held up her train. We were signaled to follow, and fell in behind, with old Atlas bringing up the rear. In procession we followed along many grand promenades and after a time arrived at the House of the Sun. There, on a specially erected and comfortably furnished dais, we were seated to watch this comedy. We all sat at the king's right, though a little apart, with our girls on the left, except those royal maidens carrying the king's emblems from the altar, who were given a special place at the top. The others had to make do standing below between the columns.

The comedy[15] we were shown had some really remarkable things in it, so I will outline briefly what it was about.

ACT ONE: First of all a very old king comes on with his servants, and a little chest is brought out that we're told was

....

15 It's common in older literature to interpolate a story within the story that tells a reflected or reversed or otherwise altered version of the events in the main story. Montgomery interprets the events in the play as both an allegory of the alchemical Work *and* as Christian and Biblical allegories representing ("of course") the Covenant of God and Israel, the stages of history in the Book of Daniel, the appearance of Jesus, his rejection by the world, etc. Even a brief analysis of the play as an allegory of the Work would have to be lengthy and could be disputed. Orphans, king's sons, love, loss, death, reanimation, exaltation, degradation, further loss, and final redemption and marriage can (of course) be found in thousands of stories.

rescued from the sea. It's opened, and inside is a beautiful baby girl, together with some jewels and a letter for the king. He reads it and weeps. He tells his servants that long before, the king of the Moors invaded lands belonging to a kinswoman of his, to whose daughter the king had betrothed his own son. The Moor killed all her offspring, right down to this little child, the only one to escape. So the king swears enmity against the Moor and vows revenge. He orders the child to be cared for and war prepared against the Moor. The rest of the act was taken up with this, and with the girl's education (she is put under the care of an elderly tutor), along with other entertaining inventions.

Then an INTERLUDE: A fight between a lion and a gryphon. The lion won, and it was an exciting match to watch.

In the SECOND ACT the Moor[16] appears, a treacherous black fellow, furious at learning his murders have been discovered and that the baby girl has been stolen from him and rescued by the king. How is he to defeat this powerful adversary? He gets advice from some fugitives from the King's lands, escaping a famine. Well, his plots work, and contrary to all our expectations, the girl, now a young lady, falls again into his hands. He intends to have her strangled, but his own servants cleverly deceive him and hide

....

16 Like the old king, the Moor is an analogue of a character in the main story, one who is about to appear, with a different though similarly violent function.

her. The act ends with a splendid Moorish extravaganza.

The THIRD ACT: A great army of the king's, under the command of a valiant old knight, descends on the Moor's country and eventually rescues the young lady from the tower where she has been hidden, and puts her royal robes back on. A splendid platform is raised all in a moment and the lady elevated on it. Enter twelve royal ambassadors, and the elderly knight makes a speech saying that his king not only rescued her from death and raised her to be a princess (though she hasn't always behaved as properly as she might have),[17] but has chosen her to wed his son, if she and he swear to certain conditions. And here the knight orders a number of precepts to be read out from a scroll, all of them admirable, I would have noted them down if they hadn't been so long. The young lady swears to the conditions and thanks the knight for this high favor, after which the praises of God, the king, and the lady are sung, and everyone exits.

SECOND INTERLUDE. The four beasts[18] mentioned in the Book

....

17 The most interesting thing about the play is how the heroine swerves from standard romance heroines and exhibits a dangerous sexuality, willfulness, and lack of steadfast virtue. If the play *is* an allegory of the Work, she'd most resemble the Mercury/Cupid figure who is degraded, dies, blackens (*nigredo*), and is reborn tamed, only to lapse and suffer more degradation before the final exaltation.

18 The beasts seen in Daniel's vision in the Biblical Book of Daniel:

of Daniel, exactly as he saw them in his vision, were all brought in, each with its mystic significance.

In the FOURTH ACT, the young lady is restored to her lost kingdom, and crowned. For a while she promenades in the royal courtyards, shown around with great joy. Many ambassadors present themselves, not only to wish her well but also just to look on her in her glory. She maintains her dignity for a while, but then begins to gaze around her, gives the ambassadors and the other lords the eye and winks and flirts openly with them – the actress played all this to the life. The Moor learns of this wanton behavior and sees his chance. The princess's steward fails to watch her carefully, and she is easily swayed by the Moor's sweet talk. She secretly gives in to him, falls under his spell, and forgets about the king. The Moor makes the most of this, and having got her into his hands, he talks her into yielding control of her whole kingdom to him. In the third scene, he has her led out first to be stripped stark naked and then tied to a post on a lowly wooden platform and

....

A beast like a lion with eagle's wings; a beast like a bear with three ribs between its teeth; a beast like a leopard with four wings and four heads; lastly a beast with iron teeth and ten horns. These were commonly images of the successive ages of human history, and Protestant theologians of Andreae's day commonly thought that the fourth and last age was about to end, and conflated these beasts with the beasts of Revelations.

whipped. Then she is sentenced to death! This was so affecting that many of us wept. Naked as she is, she is thrown in prison to await her death by poison. The poison doesn't actually kill her, but it does cause her to break out in leprous sores. So this act ends rather tragically.

Another Interlude followed. A statue or figure of Nebuchadnezzar[19] was brought out, with heraldic signs of many kinds on his head, feet, legs, breast, and belly, all of which will be eventually explained.

Fifth Act: The king's son is told of everything that has happened between the Moor and his future wife. He begs his father to take action on her behalf and not leave her in that situation, so the king orders his ambassadors off to bring her whatever comfort they can in her sickness and bondage, and at the same time to scold her for her bad behavior. She refuses to receive them, and not only that, she's going to go on being the concubine of the Moor! The young prince is told of everything that has happened so far.

Interlude: A band of clowns tumbled in, each carrying a piece of something, which they rapidly assembled into a great globe of the world, and just as quickly they took it all apart again – an amusing fantasy.

....

19 The king in whose court Daniel had his dream of the four beasts.

In the Sixth Act the prince goes into battle with the Moor. The Moor is defeated, and everyone believes the prince has also been killed. He recovers, though, frees the princess, and gives her into the care of his steward and his chaplain. The steward at first lords it over the princess and torments her, but then the priest decides *he* wants a turn and is so wicked he wrests all power from the steward.[20] Word of all this reaches the prince, who sends someone who breaks that priest's grip for good and then re-dresses the princess richly (but modestly) for her wedding.

After this act a huge mechanical elephant came forth, carrying a tower on his back crowded with musicians, and this too was a big hit.

In the Last Act the bridegroom appears with such pomp you couldn't believe it, and I was astonished how they could bring it all off. The bride comes forward in the same solemn glory to meet him. (Everyone present cried out at this – *Long live the bridegroom! Long live the bride!* – so that by cheering the comedy they also congratulated our young king and queen in the neatest way, which I noticed seemed to please them very much.) The prince and his lady circled the stage, and at last

....

20 Perhaps a reference to the struggle of the Holy Roman Emperor and the Pope. Or just melodrama.

everyone began to sing this song:

Oh happy day, and blessed night!
Let all here present sing –
Joy to all who see this sight,
The wedding of the king!

O lovely bride so long awaited,
Now at last betrothed to be!
Our yearning hearts at last are sated:
For this we've striven faithfully!

We, virtuous maids and elders wise,
We've loved you and we wish you well.
May from your lawful pairing rise
Descendants more than tongue can tell!

There were thanks then from everyone to everyone, and the comedy, which must have been particularly delightful for the royal persons, was over.

Evening was coming on, and we all departed in order as before, up the long winding stair and into the hall I described, where tables were lavishly laid. This was the first time we were invited to dine in the company of the king. The little altar was set down in the middle of the hall, and the six royal emblems placed on it again.

The young king was very gracious, but he seemed unable to be happy; now and then he would exchange some words with us, then look away and sigh – for which little Cupid made fun of him, and tried to tease him. The old king and the old queen were also very serious; only the young wife of the old king was at all happy, for a reason I didn't yet understand. There were three tables: the royal persons at the first, at the second just we brothers, and at the third some of the royal maidens; the rest of the girls and others had to serve. Everything was done with great state, but in such solemn silence that I'm afraid to write much about it. I can say that before the meal began all the kings and queens dressed themselves in snow-white shining garments and then sat down. Over their table hung the great golden crown, whose brilliant gems could have lit the hall all by themselves, but candles filled the hall – all of them lit from the small taper on the altar: what the reason for that was I don't at all know. I certainly did notice that the young king several times sent a bit of food to the white serpent, and that required thinking about.

Almost all the chatter at the banquet was little Cupid's. He couldn't leave us (and especially me) alone, but kept bringing up odd topics and producing surprises. He couldn't arouse much laughter, though; the meal went on in silence, which made me, at least, think that something dreadful was in the offing. There was no music; anyone who was asked a question gave a short, distracted answer that offered no conversation. In short, everything had such a sinister aspect that the sweat began trickling down my sides, and I really think that even the bravest man might have felt nervous.

by Christian Rosencreutz 133

Now the supper was almost over, and the king ordered the book to be handed to him from the altar. He opened it before him and had an aged courtier ask us once again if we were all resolved to stand by him, in prosperity and in adversity. We said, trembling, that we would, and he asked gravely whether we would sign our names to that pledge, and we of course had no choice but to say yes, and one after another we got up and each with his own hand wrote his name in the book.

When this was done, the little crystal ever-flowing fountain was brought forward, along with a tiny crystal glass. The royals drank the blood-red fluid, one after the other, and then it was given to us, and then to everyone present. It was called the Drink of Silence. All the royal persons gave us their hands and said that if we didn't stick by them this night, we'd never see them ever again, which brought tears to our eyes. Our directress stood up for us and promised eloquently on our behalf, which gratified them.

Just then a bell tolled, and at the sound the faces of all the royals turned so incredibly bleak that we were close to despair. Quickly they took off their white garments, revealing their black ones beneath. The whole hall was then hung with black velvet, even the ceiling – all this having been prepared in advance.[21] We also were given black robes to put

....

21 The royals are again in black, shedding their innocent white, and the whole room is in black – both funereal and appropriate to the *nigredo* stage of alchemy.

on. The tables were removed, and everyone seated themselves along the dais. Our president, who had slipped out of the hall, now returned bringing six black satin scarves, with which she blindfolded the six royal persons. As soon as they were unable to see, six covered coffins were brought in by the servants and set down in the hall, and a low black bench was placed in the middle.

Then there came into the hall a very tall man, black as coal, who carried a large and very sharp axe. The old king was brought to kneel at the bench, and without a moment's hesitation the black man lopped off his head! The head was wrapped in black cloth, and the gushing blood was caught in a great golden chalice and placed with the old king, and the old king's head, in his coffin, which was covered again.

It went the same with each of the others in turn, so that I began to think that maybe my turn would come too, but no, as soon as the six royals were beheaded, the black man stalked out again. But just outside the door, apparently, someone beheaded *him*, for his head and his axe were brought back in, and they were put into a small chest.

This was a bloody wedding! I had no idea what was to happen, and I tried to suspend judgment until I understood better. Our lady, seeing that some of us were weakening and weeping, told us to pull ourselves together. "The lives of these six[22] are in

....

22 This is in fact the last we'll see of the old king and the middle-aged king and their spouses; their essences will eventually form part of

your hands," she said. "Do as I tell you and these deaths will mean life for many."

She made it clear that we should now just go off to bed, and not grieve for them, for they would get all that they deserved in the end. She said good-night to us all; she herself had to keep watch over the bodies nightlong.

We could only obey. Our pages conducted us to our rooms. My page talked to me of this and that, and I actually remember much that he said – it gave me reason to admire his mind – but I came to see that his real intention was simply to lull me to sleep after the events of the evening. At last I did pretend to fall asleep. But I wasn't asleep at all; I couldn't put the images of those beheadings out of my mind.

My room was over the bay, and I could look out across it from the windows beside my bed. At midnight, on the stroke of twelve, I saw what seemed to be a fire on the water. I threw open the shutters. Seven ships were approaching across the bay, all lit up. Above each of them hovered a tongue of flame, coming and passing, sometimes descending to the deck: and somehow it was obvious to me that these were the spirits of the beheaded men and women. Soundlessly the ships came to shore, and I could see that each was crewed by a single sailor. When they had tied up, I saw our mistress, with a torch, going toward them, and behind her were carried the six covered coffins, and the small chest. Each of them was taken aboard a

....

the royal pair's revival.

ship and hidden below.

I awakened my page, who was very glad of it, because he'd been running around all day long and might well have slept through this event, which he knew all about. All the coffins had now been taken aboard, the running lights were put out, and the six tongues of flame[23] passed together back across the bay. A

....

23 This episode poses a few problems. Seven ships come over the bay from Olympus Tower accompanied by flames, and Christian understands they are the spirits of the beheaded people. The coffins of the royals and the box containing the Moor's head are then each put aboard a ship. Then all the lights on the ships are put out. Six of the seven tongues of flame pass back over the bay to the tower. Do six of the ships also go back, bearing the six coffins of the royals, unload the coffins at the tower, and then come back to where the soldiers guard the shore? Or do the ships, with the coffins stowed aboard, wait for morning to go all together to the tower island? In the original, a marginal note in Latin says *Cadavera avehuntur trans lacus* – "The bodies are carried across the lake." What then becomes of the seventh flame? Montgomery has a rather tortured argument that it is the spirit of Venus, in whose chamber the dead royals spent the hours between beheading and trans-shipping, but I can't see it. If it's the spirit of the Moor, it apparently stays with him on the ship, but why is it no longer seen? If the spirit-flames don't accompany the bodies back across the water, what is their function? It may be, of course, that the "six" is simply an error, Andreae's or a typesetter's. I've left it as the literal translation states it. More complications of this (probably

single night-lamp was lit on each ship. We could see now that hundreds of guards were preparing to camp that night on the shore, and they sent our mistress back to the castle. She bolted the doors and gates again with care. I could see that nothing more would happen this night; we would have to wait till day.

So we two went back to bed. I was the only one of my brethren who had a room facing the bay, so I was the only one who saw this: and now, completely exhausted, I fell at last asleep in the midst of a thousand thoughts.

....

unresolvable) problem will appear on the following day.

The Fifth Day

The night was passed, and the dear longed-for day had just broken,
when I leapt out of bed, more eager to find out what was going
to happen next than I was to go on sleeping. I put on my clothes,
and as before I slipped down the stairs, but it was still too early
and the hall was empty. I returned then, and asked my page if
he would please take me around the castle for a bit and show me
something special. He was agreeable (as he always was), and he
led me down a certain staircase that led down under the earth.
We came to a great iron door, and set into the door were tall letters, made of copper.[1] They said:

ID?p 8?gq Dpgsxdpö
d?p b>höö ?sxu,Bööxöɔhpö
VENVS.
Höpöö₁ö
uödg8ú>k,phs.bpgpövo6 wöɡɟxsg
gpdsxɔhg hxgg.[2]

....

1 In alchemy, copper is the metal of Venus as lead is of Saturn and iron of
Mars. Venus is a key but ambiguous figure in the alchemical process – she
can symbolize both the unclean and chaotic matter with which the alchemist begins his work – she is referred to as the Whore – but she can also
be the cold, chaste, moist substance related to the Moon and to silver.

2 The letters are a simple substitution code, with odd symbols

I copied this inscription down in my notebook. We opened the door, and my page led me through a dark passage till we came to another door, this one very small, which was not fully closed. "This door was opened yesterday,"[3] my page said, "when the six coffins were taken out, and hasn't yet been shut."

As soon as we went in, I beheld the most amazing thing Nature has ever produced, for the vault was lit by nothing but a number of immense jewels – this was, my page said, the king's treasury! A tomb stood in the middle of the place, so fabulously rich I was amazed it was left unguarded.

"You should thank your lucky stars," my page said. "You are getting to see things that no other human has ever laid eyes on, except the royal family themselves."

This tomb was triangular. In the middle of it stood a large polished copper basin. The rest was pure gold and gems. In the copper basin stood an angel who held in her arms the branches of an unearthly tree which dropped fruit continuously into the basin. As soon as a fruit touched the water it became water itself and flowed away into three smaller vessels nearby. The whole thing was supported by three animals: an

....

standing for letters in German. It's mere mystification, since the page translates a moment later.

3 The events are occurring in linkage with one another, truly resembling the cascade of events in an alchemical athenor. Venus is in the cold state preceding the beginning of the Work to revive the dead royals.

eagle, an ox, and a lion, standing on a splendid base.[4]

"What does all this mean?" I asked.

"It means," he said (as had the door we passed through), "that *here Lady Venus lies, the beauty who's undone so many and robbed them of wealth, honor, blessing, and happiness.*" Then he pointed to a copper door, let into the paving-stones of the vault. "If you want, we can go down farther."

"I'll follow you," I said.

He lifted the door, and I went down the steps after him. It was pitch dark, but in a moment he opened a little box that held an ever-burning candle, and at it he lit one of the torches that lay there. I was growing extremely nervous, and I asked him very seriously if we should be doing this.

"As long as all the royal persons are still asleep, we don't need to be afraid."

In the room we reached was a rich bed, hung about with exquisitely embroidered curtains. We drew the curtains aside, and *I saw Lady Venus.* My page pulled off her coverlets, and there she was, stark naked,[5] lying in such beauty, such an

....

4 The eagle, the ox and the lion are Christian symbols of three of the four Gospels. They are also three of the beasts who draw the car of Ezekiel to the throne of God. The fourth would be a winged man, who could be the central angel described here, except that this figure is explicitly female. The mystery isn't lessened by the Page's bland answer to Christian's question – it's just the translation of the coded copper letters.

5 Montgomery notes the resemblance of the whole scene to the Tarot

astonishment, that I was almost beside myself. I couldn't tell if perhaps she was actually a piece of carven stone, or a human dead body, she was so entirely still and unmoving – I didn't dare touch her to find out. At last he covered her again and drew the curtain; yet she had been imprinted, so to speak, on my eyes, and I saw her still.

Beside the bed was a tablet, with these words written on it:

I asked my page what *this* meant, but he just laughed and promised that I'd find out myself soon enough. He put out the

....

card called The World (XXI), showing a naked woman surrounded by the four animals of Ezekiel/the Gospels. What if anything the correspondence might signify can't be known, as we have no knowledge that Andreae had any interest in or knowledge of Tarot; Tarot trumps weren't commonly used as occult symbols until a later century.

6 "When the fruit of my tree/Shall be entirely/Molten I will/Awake and be/A mother of a/King." Again, the page will respond in a moment by translating the coded letters.

torch, and we climbed out again. Now I could have a better look around in the vault, and discovered a number of small alcoves, and in each a little pyrite taper was burning – I hadn't noticed this before, because the flame of the taper was so clear and steady that it resembled a jewel more than a flame. But these pyrite tapers were causing the fruit-tree that the angel held to melt away, even though it continued to produce new fruit.

"Here's what I heard old Atlas tell the king," my page said to me. "When the tree is entirely melted away, that's when Lady Venus down below is going to wake up, become the mother of a king…"[7]

Perhaps he was going to tell me more, but just then little Cupid flew into the room. At first he seemed alarmed to find the two of us there, but when he saw how pale and stunned we ourselves were, more like the dead than the living, he had to laugh. "What ghost brought *you* here?" he asked me.

"I got lost in the castle," I stammered. "Somehow, I don't know how, I ended up here. This page, my page, went looking for me everywhere, and just now has come upon me here. I hope I haven't done anything wrong."

"Well, all right, my busy old grandpa," Cupid responded. "But you might have played a mean trick on me, if you'd guessed what this door here is for. I'd better just lock it up." And he put a big lock on the copper door I'd gone down by.

Thank God he hadn't found me sooner! My page was relieved too that I'd covered for him in a pinch.

....

7 The page attributes the mystic words to old Atlas.

...I saw Lady Venus.

"And yet, and yet," said Cupid, still smiling. "I don't think I can just let you off, seeing how close you came to stumbling on dear Mother." With that, he thrust the point of his dart into the flame of one of the bright pyrite tapers, and when it was hot he pricked me with it on the palm of my hand. It didn't hurt too badly at the time – I was just glad that I'd got away with so little harm done. Or so I thought.[8]

Meantime everyone else had risen and gone down into the hall, so I snuck up to my room and then came back down again, as though I too had just awakened. Cupid, when he'd locked up those secret chambers below, came in too. He made me show him my hand, where there was still a little drop of blood. "Better be nice to him," he joked to the others. "He's not long for this world!" It amazed all of us that Cupid could flit about so cheerfully, without any sense of the dreadful things that happened the day before – he seemed entirely untroubled.

Our president appeared, dressed for a journey in black velvet, but carrying her laurel branch as always. Everything was prepared, she said; we were to drink something and then quickly form up for the procession, so we drank and followed her in order out into the court.

....

8 This moment with Cupid is the crux of one theme of the story, a theme or series of events that stands in a counterpoint with the triumphant story of the re-creation of the royal couple. Both are centrally about sex, but one is the inverse of the other.

There lay six coffins. All my brothers of course assumed that the six royal persons were inside them. I knew better, but I didn't know what the point was of these six empty ones.[9] By each coffin stood eight hooded men. As soon as music was heard – awesomely tragic and dreary – the men lifted the coffins, and we went after them into that same garden where we had seen the unweighty people punished. A wooden pavilion had been set up there, standing on seven pillars and topped with a crown. Within it were dug six graves, and by each one was a slab of stone, but in the middle was a large hollow stone globe. Silently and gravely the coffins were lowered into the graves and the stones were laid over them and sealed. The little chest containing the head and axe of the black executioner – supposedly – was placed in the round stone in the middle.

My companions were all completely fooled. They could only suppose that the royal corpses were now entombed. A large flag with a phoenix painted on it was raised above the building, perhaps to make monkeys of us all the better, I don't know[10] – I was

....

9 Starting here, certain of the brothers are going to be variously fooled and misdirected, so that only a small number end up participating in the culmination of the work.

10 The Phoenix is periodically consumed in fire and then resurrects itself from its own ashes. A very common symbol throughout alchemical lore (and Christian iconography) of life arising from death. The brothers are able to read the symbol, which will add to their certainty that the bodies to be resurrected are buried below.

just grateful to God that I knew more than the others did.

When all these ceremonies were done, our mistress climbed up to stand on top of the stone globe. She spoke briefly, telling us that we should fulfill the commitments we had made, not shrink from the suffering and labor we must undergo but pitch in to bring these royal persons buried here back to life. "Rise up now, and come with me to Olympus Tower, to bring back the necessary life-giving medicines!"

Of course we all cried out that we would, and she led us out through a little door in the courtyard that opened right onto the shore. There were the seven ships, all empty.[11] Our president's troop of girls had planted their own laurel branches on the ships' decks, and they assigned each of us to one or another of them. When we were all aboard, the ships were commanded in the name of God to set out. From the shore those maidens watched us till they could see us no more, and then with the guards returned into the castle.

Each of our ships had a great banner and was marked with its own sign. Five of the signs were the five Platonic solids, and my ship, on which the lady president also sailed, had the sign of the sphere. Each ship had only two crewmen, and we sailed in a particular order. In front went the small ship in which I guessed the Moor's head lay, and which also carried twelve fine musicians. Its

....

11 This too suggests that the bodies have already been transported to the island; but in the next paragraph Christian guesses that the Moor's head is still in the lead ship. So they aren't all empty.

sign was the Pyramid. Behind that ship three sailed abreast, and mine was the middle one. Behind us came the two tallest and grandest ships, decorated with many of the laurel branches and carrying no passengers; their flags were the Sun and the Moon.[12] In the rear was one ship, carrying forty of the royal maidens.

We crossed the wide bay and out through a channel into the sea itself,[13] and what did we see but all the sirens, sea-goddesses, nymphs and mermaids waiting for us! They sent one mermaid swimming over to deliver a present from all of them in honor of the wedding. It was a huge pearl, glowing and perfectly round, in a rich setting, a pearl the like of which has never been seen, not in our hemisphere, and not in the New World, either. Our directress received it.

"Would you all," this mermaid asked, "like to stop your ships here for a while, and let us entertain you?"

"Very gladly," our president called down to her.

She gave directions that the two tall ships flying the Sun and Moon should stand in the middle of a pentagon formed by the rest of us. The sirens and nymphs formed a ring around us and with the most delicate, sweet, piercing voices began to sing this song:

....

12 These two ships ought to be carrying the coffins containing the king and queen; if they were transported the night before (see above), the imposture about the coffins is continuing.

13 In alchemy, the undifferentiated *prima materia* the Work begins with. One alchemical text says the dead king must be marinated in the sea before being brought to dry land.

What can be, on earth or sea,
More lovely than true love?
It makes us good as good can be,
To neighbors each more neighborly.
So let's all sing, unto the king,
So loud the sky and sea shall ring:
We'll ask, and all you answer!

What gives sweet life to all?
(It's love!)
What lifts us when we fall?
(It's love!)

We're from our mothers born –
Through love;
Without it live forlorn –
Dear love!
Man lies in bliss with wife –
It's love!
Babe sucks her breast for life –
That's love!

What to our parents do we owe?
Love, all love.
What makes them patient with us so?
It's their good love.

What can overcome the worst?
It's love!
How do we find such love at first?
Through love!

So let's all sing, our song resounding –
In our queen and our true king
Love with love by love increasing.
Their bodies earthly, souls of fire,
We'll labor, suffer, never tire,
By God's great name, by His love's flame,
We'll join them each to each again.

By the time they had finished this song, so heart-shaking in
its harmonies and melodies, I understood why Ulysses stopped
the ears of his shipmates – I felt like the unluckiest man alive,
simply because I was myself and not a creature as lovely and
blessed as these. But the young mistress soon sent them away
and commanded us to sail on. She sent to the mermaids a long
red scarf for a reward, and they all dispersed into the sea.

Well, I was coming to be very aware that Cupid had begun
his work inside me, which wasn't really my doing, I suppose.
Since any lengthy description of these giddy feelings I felt
isn't going to do the reader any good, I won't go into details. I
understood, though, that the hurt I'd taken from Cupid was
prophesied by the wound to my head I got in the dungeon
of my dream on that first day. Let me warn you, then, about

hanging around by Venus's bed: her son Cupid's not going to let it pass unpunished!

We spent the rest of the time aboard in pleasant talk, and at length came in sight of Olympus Tower. The young mistress ordered some cannons fired to announce our approach, and almost immediately we saw a great white flag raised over the tower, and a little gilded craft set out to meet us. When it came close, we could see a very elderly man aboard, who was the warder of the tower, and guards dressed in white.[14] We were hailed in friendship and our ships were conducted to the tower harbor.

The tower stood upon a perfectly square island and was surrounded by a wall so thick that I counted two hundred and sixty steps in passing through it. Past the wall was a pleasant meadow, with here and there small orchards where exotic fruits – unknown at least to me – were ripening; then an inner wall circling the tower itself. The tower resembled seven separate towers bound together, with the middle one a little higher; inside, they let into one another, and each was seven stories high. As soon as we entered in at the gate, we were ushered

....

14 The white clothes and the white flag can be understood as suggesting the *albedo* stage of the work, when the blackened corpse of matter has been washed in mercurial waters and turned white. Seas and white flags and seven-story towers and the phoenix are common in allegorical tales of things that happen in alchemical experiments – but it seems to me that *CW* can't be an allegory of the alchemical work and a straightforward recounting of it at the same time.

away down to one side – obviously this was so that the cof-fins[15] could be brought in without our seeing them, though of course no one else knew that.

We were taken down into the very bottom of the tower, which was painted with striking murals but was very sparely furnished – basically it was a laboratory, where we were to crush and wash herbs and precious stones and other sorts of things and extract their essences, and bottle these and store them. Our young mistress bustled among us giving orders and making sure everyone had plenty to do; we were to be mere laborers here until we had done all that was necessary for the restoring of those beheaded bodies. I learned afterwards that as we worked, three of her girls were washing the bodies with care in a nearby chamber.

When we had worked a good long time, we were given a little broth and a small glass of wine, and nothing more, which made it clear we weren't here for pleasure. At the end of our day of labor everyone had to be satisfied with only a thin mattress, laid on the floor, to sleep on. I myself didn't care about sleep-ing; I went out into the garden, and went as far as the outer wall. The night was perfectly clear, and I was happy to spend

....

15 This sentence compounds the mystery of when the coffins arrive – it seems to say distinctly that the brothers are taken to one side so that the coffins can be secretly unloaded, though this ought to have happened the night before if they were all brought over then. Montgomery says simply "This took place the previous night," without explaining how.

the time watching the stars. I happened upon a set of stone stairs leading to the top of the wall, and the moonlight was so bright that I dared go up them, and stood looking out at the sea, which was now quite calm.

When I had oriented myself and studied the sky more thoroughly, I realized that on this very night an unusual conjunction of the planets could be observed. I had been thus looking out at sea for a good while, when just at midnight, as the tower clock struck twelve, I saw far-off the seven flames.[16] They were coming over the sea, toward the island, headed it seemed for the midmost tower. I grew afraid, for as soon as the flames had gathered at the tower's top, the wind rose, and the sea grew stormy; clouds covered the moon, and my enjoyment turned to terror. I scarcely had time to find the stairs by which I'd come up, and get down into the tower again. Whether the seven flames remained there at the tower's top or went away again, I can't say, because in the dark and the wind I didn't dare go out again. I lay down on my mattress on the laboratory floor beside a gently murmuring fountain, and with that I fell asleep.

So the fifth day, too, ended with amazing events.

....

16 Now they are seven again, and they are coming to the tower from across the water, apparently from the castle (where else?) Where have they been, doing what?

The Sixth Day

Next morning, after we had awakened one another, we sat on our mattresses for a while and talked about what we thought might be going on and what might be yet to come. Some of us believed that the royal ones would all be brought back to life together; others said no, the death of the older ones would restore the life of the younger ones, but would also increase it. Others guessed that they hadn't been executed at all, and that others had somehow been beheaded in their places.

We'd been talking for a while when the old warder came in and greeted us. He looked at all we'd done the day before to see if everything had been completed just so. We had worked well and thoroughly, and he could find nothing wrong, so he put all the glass jars containing our products into a case.

After a while a number of young men came in bringing some ladders, some lengths of rope, and some pairs of wings.

"My dear boys," the warder said to us. "Each one of you will have to carry one of these three things with you through the day. You can each choose which one you want, or you can distribute them among you by lot."

We all replied that we'd like to choose ourselves, but he immediately said, "No. No, we'll do it by lot."

He made three little cards, and wrote on them "Ladder" or

"Rope" or "Wings" and put them in a hat. Each of us had to draw, and whatever you got you were stuck with. Those who got the ropes thought they were the lucky ones; I happened to draw "Ladder," which was going to be a lot of trouble, since the ladder was twelve feet long and very heavy. The ones with the ropes could just coil them over their shoulders, and as for the wings, the warder stuck them onto the backs of those who'd drawn them, and there they stayed as though they'd grown them.

He turned off a tap at the fountain to stop it flowing, and we had to move it out of the way, and after everything was put away he left, taking the case full of jars, and locked the door behind him – we could only think we'd been imprisoned there. A quarter of an hour passed, and then suddenly a door covering a circular opening in the ceiling above was lifted, and who should look down on us but our own young mistress.

"Good morning," she said. "Come on up!"

This was easy enough for those with wings – they immediately flew to the hole and through it – and we with the ladders saw now what they were for. The ones with the ropes had the hardest time, because as soon as those with the ladders reached the top we were told to pull up our ladders after us. The rope people had to fling their ropes up to catch an iron hook and pull themselves up, which resulted in plenty of blisters.

As soon as we were all up, the opening was closed again, and our mistress kindly welcomed us. The room where we found ourselves was as wide as the tower and had six pretty chambers around it, raised three steps above the room itself. We were directed into these vestries or chapels, to pray there for the lives of the king and queen. The lady herself went out a small door till we had finished.

When we had completed our prayers, twelve people came in through the small door – we recognized them as the musicians from yesterday – and placed in the middle of the room a thing – a puzzling object, somewhat *long* in shape, that my companions, I suppose, thought must be a sort of fountain or distillery. But I could tell that the royal corpses were inside it, for the oval base of the object was easily large enough to hold them one atop another. The musicians went back to get their instruments, and with oh-so-delicate music they conducted in our mistress and her attendant girls. The lady carried a casket, but the others had only branches and little lamps – though some brought lighted torches, which they gave to us. We were all to stand around this fountain in the following order: First, the young mistress, at *A*, with her attendants, c, carrying branches and lamps. Then ourselves, b, with torches; then the musicians, also at a, in a long row; then last some other girls, d, in a long row too. (Where these other girls came from, if they lived in the tower or had somehow been brought in at night, I didn't know, for all their faces were covered with white veils, and I couldn't identify them.)

```
oooooooo a
     ooooo
  ooooooooo
c  o  O  o  b
  o     o
 ooo A ooo
   ooooo
oooooooo d
```

The young mistress opened her casket and took out a round

thing wrapped up in a piece of green changeable taffeta. She laid this in the small top chamber of the object and then covered it with the lid, which was pierced with holes. The lid had a deep rim into which she poured several of the liquids we had prepared yesterday, and immediately the fountain started running. The maiden attendants stuck their lamps on points that surrounded the lower container, so as to heat the liquid. When it boiled, the fountain or still[1] drew the liquid back up through the pierced lid into the small vessel and out through four pipes onto the bodies concealed within the large container. The liquids were now so hot that they would melt the bodies inside and reduce them to a kind of liquor. What I knew – but my companions didn't – was that the round thing the lady had placed in the upper vessel was the head of the black executioner, and that head was what caused the super-heating of the fluids drawn up over it. The maidens carrying branches stuck them into holes in the great oval vessel; this might have been purely ceremonial, I don't know, but some of the fluid running down into the large vessel spurted out the holes and over the branches, and then dripped back down in again, seeming somehow more brightly yellow.

....

1 A. E. Waite, a scholar of the occult and an early publisher of *CW* in a modern version, calls this description "a confused text," and indeed it is hard to discern how the thing is supposed to work. That the liquid heated by the lamps around the vessel where the bodies are is percolating up around the Moor's head, being reheated there, and running back down, is my best guess.

This distillation and melting lasted nearly two hours, the still running constantly on its own, though the longer it ran the weaker its action grew. Meanwhile the musicians went away, and we walked up and down in that room. It was easy to kill time there, filled as the place was with images, paintings, automata, organs, circulating fountains and similar wonders. When the still slowed to a stop and wouldn't percolate any longer, the young mistress sent for a hollow golden globe to be brought. She opened a tap at the bottom of the large oval vessel and let all the matter that had been dissolved or liquefied by the boiling fluids – some of it deep red – run into the hollow globe. (The remaining fluid in the top vessel was discarded.) The whole object then was removed, and was obviously much lighter than it had been; whether it was taken somewhere and opened up, whether anything usable remained of the bodies that had been inside, I just don't know. But I do know that the liquid that filled the globe was too heavy for six and more of us to lift, though by the size of it you'd think one person could have carried it easily. Anyway it was carried out through the door with a lot of effort, and we were once again left all alone. Overhead I could hear the sound of footsteps, and I remembered my ladder and got a grip on it.

It was interesting listening to the opinions of my companions about that fountain or distillery and its action, for of course they supposed that the royal corpses were buried in the earth of the garden in the castle, and had no idea what had gone on here; I was again thankful that I'd awakened on that night and seen what I'd seen – it was helping me in carrying out our mistress's great task.

After a few minutes, an opening in the ceiling of this chamber was uncovered, as I had suspected it would be. The young mistress looked down on us and ordered us all to come up, and we did it the same way as before – wings, ladders, ropes. I was a little annoyed that her handmaids could go upstairs by another way, and we had to expend so much effort, but I guessed there must be some good reason for it; handing them out and seeing to their use at least gave the old warder something to do in this process, but even those he'd given wings to only had that momentary advantage when they had to go up through the opening.

When I got up, and the opening had been shut behind me, I saw that the golden globe was hanging by a strong golden chain in the middle of the chamber. There was nothing else in the room but the windows. Between each pair of windows was a brilliantly polished mirror with a door that could be closed over it. These mirrors were angled in such a way that when the windows on the side of the room the sun shone in on were opened, and the doors covering the mirrors were opened too, the light of the sun (which was in itself terrifically bright this morning) was reflected around so that the whole room was nothing but suns! The refracted light and heat were focused on the golden globe hanging in the center, whose surface was also highly polished, so what with the light everywhere you couldn't even look at it, and we had to stare out the windows instead while the globe was heated to the right degree. I'll say it again, on my honor – this was the most amazing spectacle of light that Nature could produce – there were suns everywhere, in every corner, and the golden globe was even brighter, and you could no more look right at it than you can look at the sun itself for more than a blink.

The young mistress at length ordered the mirrors to be covered and the windows to be shuttered, to let the globe cool down a little. It was about seven o'clock now, and we were glad of it, thinking we might have time now for some breakfast. Well, what we got you might call a philosopher's breakfast, "nothing in excess" for sure, though we weren't left hungry. And the hope of great happiness later on – which the young lady often held out to us – made us forget any inconveniences and frets. I truly can say, about all my good companions, that they weren't men whose thoughts dwelled much on their dinners; what they really wanted was to continue on this adventure in science and by means of it to contemplate the Creator's wisdom and power.

After we'd eaten, we went back to work. The globe was cool enough now that we could lift it off its chain, which was no mean feat. Then we discussed how to divide it in half – which is what we were told we had to do – and decided that a sharp-pointed diamond might work best, which in the end it did. What was inside it was not red at all but white: a beautiful large white egg. We were so glad that it had come out well, because our mistress had been very worried that the shell might still be too thin and soft. We stood around this egg as pleased as if we'd laid it ourselves. But quickly the lady ordered it taken away, and followed it herself, and (as before) the door was locked on us. What she did elsewhere with that egg, whether it was treated in some way secretly, I don't know, but I don't believe so. At any rate there we were alone again and waiting till the opening to the fourth floor[2] was uncovered, to which we got up by our different means.

In this room we found a great copper basin filled with yellow sand, which was warmed by a gentle fire. The egg was laid in it and the sand raked over it, so it could complete its incubation. This copper thing was square; on one side these two verses were inscribed in large letters:

O. BLI. TO. BIT. MI. LI.
KANT. I. VOLT. BIT. TO. GOLT.

On another side were these three words:

SANITAS. NIX. HASTA.

The third side had only one word:

F. I. A. T.[3]

2 It should by now be apparent that brothers are making their way up one story at each stage of the process till the seventh floor is reached.
3 A modern German commentator expands these abbreviations into a

But on the back was a whole inscription:

THAT WHICH
Fire. Air. Water. Earth.
Were not able to strip from
The ashes of
OUR SACRED KING AND QUEEN
Was gathered by the faithful flock
Of Alchemists
In this vessel.[4]

....

Latin phrase: *Obligatio tolle bitumen minutum liquefactumque kantione ignique voltus bituminis tollitur golt.* This would mean "You must take pulverized and liquefied bitumen and with fire and music [?] change the form of the bitumen to gold." If this is right, it still doesn't tell us its meaning in context. Bitumen is a black, oily product of the breakdown of organic compounds like petroleum – basically, tar. SANITAS. NIX. HASTA: I have seen no good explanation for this. "Sanitas" means health. "Hasta" is a spear. Montgomery connects it to a passage in Book XII of Vergil's *Aeneid*, in which a wise physician cures Aeneas as he stands leaning on his spear ("nixus in hastam"). F. I. A. T.: "Let [it] be done [or made]," as in the opening line of *Genesis: Fiat lux*, "let there be light." As an acronym, it remains obscure (to me; others have offered expansions they espouse).

4 The appearance of this inscription on the egg-box implies, even makes certain, that the ceremony of the death and rebirth of the king has happened many times. See below, note to the last page.

I leave it to the experts to decide if this meant the egg, or the sand it was put in; I'm just trying not to leave anything out. That egg was ready now, and was taken out, but it didn't need to be cracked, for the bird inside it quickly broke out by himself, and he seemed to be very glad indeed to be out, though actually he looked rather bloody and unformed. We placed him on the warm sand, and the young mistress warned us to tie him up securely or he'd soon be giving us endless trouble. We did that, and then his food was brought in – which was certainly nothing but the blood of the beheaded royal persons, diluted with the waters we had prepared. You could actually see the bird grow from drinking it, so fast that we could understand why our mistress had warned us about him: he bit and scratched so strongly that if we'd let him go he'd have done for any of us he could get. He was very wild, and completely black, until some different food was brought in – maybe it was the blood of a different royal person, but as soon as he consumed it all his black feathers

....

5 One commentator decrypts this line as "A.D. 1459" – the year the events in *CW* are supposed to take place. How it comes to be already prepared and the process described on it in the past tense is hard to explain. The coded line, however, might also (if looked at just right) be symbols of the twelve astrological signs interlaced with a central symbol, the Monad, described above p. 39.

molted, and he grew snow-white[6] feathers instead. He was a little tamer too, but we didn't trust him. He got a third feeding, and this time his feathers turned the most gorgeous array of colors[7] I've ever seen, and he became so gentle and tame, and was so friendly, that our young mistress said we could untie him.

"This bird's been brought to life and raised to adulthood by your hard work and the old warder's kind permission," she said, "which is good reason for a feast in its honor."

She ordered that dinner be brought in and said we should take it easy now, since the hardest part of our job was over. We began to celebrate, even though we were still wearing our mourning clothes from the castle, which seemed to clash with the party. The young mistress was as always inquisitive, trying to find out which of us she could put to use in what way, and her talk at this dinner was mostly about Melting. She was very glad to learn that one of us turned out to be an expert in

....

6 Again, the transformation from the *nigredo* (blackened) state of the Work to the *albedo* (whitened) state. It seems to happen in the story as a continuous or repeated event or action rather than a single determinative one – like a theme in music. (See instances noted above.)

7 The "peacock" state of the Work – though most alchemical texts put this state after the *nigredo* and before the *albedo*. This is the end of the lesser stage of the Work. What remains in standard alchemical practice is the achieving of the *rubedo* or red stage, where the Red King is made and married to the White Woman; their son is the Stone of the Philosophers, able to perfect all substances.

that topic, well acquainted with the literature. We were only three-quarters of an hour at dinner, and we still had to get up in turn and feed the bird, though he had stopped growing much. Just as soon as we'd taken the last bite, the lady disappeared, taking the bird with her.

Soon the fifth floor was opened up to us, and up we went in the same way as before, ready to go to work. There was a bathtub in this room, ready for the bird, and the bathwater was infused with some white substance that made it look like milk. The liquid was cool, and when we placed the bird in it he seemed to enjoy it, splashing around gently. The lamps lit under the tub began to heat it up, though, and soon it was so hot it was hard to keep him in it; we had finally to put a cover over the bath, with a hole in it he could poke his head through, and we kept him in there until he had lost all his feathers and was as smooth as a baby. The heat didn't harm him in any other way, which I thought was remarkable, since the hot water had completely dissolved the feathers and colored the bathwater slightly blue. We uncovered the tub so the bird could get some air, and he jumped out on his own. He was so shining smooth that it was a pleasure to look at him. He was still a little wild, though, and we had to put a collar and chain around his neck to lead him up and down the room. Meanwhile a hot fire was built under the bathtub, and the liquid boiled away till it was reduced to a lump of blue stone,[8] which we took out, crushed,

....

8 Blue things are rather rare in alchemy, though Paracelsus compared

and ground to powder. We used the powder to paint the bird's naked skin all over. Now he looked really weird, because he was all blue, except for his white-feathered head.

So that was our job on that floor, and after the young mistress took away the blue bird, we were summoned up through the opening to the sixth floor.

This was a little troubling. There stood a little altar arranged exactly as the one in the king's hall in the castle. The six royal things were on it, just as I've described them, the ever-burning taper, the black book, the watch, the planetary model, the fountain of blood-red fluid, and the serpent in the skull. The blue bird now made the seventh.[9]

First he had a large drink out of the fountain. Then he pecked the serpent until she bled profusely; this blood we had to catch in a golden cup and pour down the bird's throat, which she hated and fought against. Then we had to dip the serpent's head into the fountain, which revived her, and she crept back into her skull and wasn't seen for a long time. The planetary sphere had gone on turning, and when it reached some satisfactory conjunction, the watch struck one; that caused the sphere to start turning again to make a new conjunction, until the watch struck two. We saw the sphere reach

....

the achieved Work to a sapphire. Projecting a blue color over the evolving Work is mentioned in some texts. The image of the big blue bird remains, as Christian says, mighty odd.

9 Another sequence of seven is completed.

a third conjunction, and when the watch struck three, the poor bird just laid down its head on the book and allowed us to cut it off. (We'd already decided by lot which of us was to do this task.) He didn't bleed at all, though, until we cut open his breast – and then the blood spurted out so fresh, and as clear as a fountain of rubies.[10]

We felt terrible in a way about this death, but still it seemed obvious to us that a naked dead blue bird wasn't going to be of any further use, and we shrugged it off. We moved aside the altar and helped our mistress to burn the dead body (along with a small plaque that hung nearby) in a fire she lit with the ever-burning taper, and then to purify the ashes several times and put them in a cypress-wood box.

Then a really cruel trick was played on me, I have to tell you. After we had very carefully saved all the ashes of the bird, our mistress said, "Gentlemen, here we are now in the sixth chamber. Only one remains, and when our labors there are over, we'll be returning to the castle to awaken our gracious lords and ladies. Now. I really wish I could say that all of you have behaved in such a way that I could commend you to the king and queen and see you all properly rewarded. But I'm afraid I've identified four lazy sluggards among you."

Here she pointed out three of the company – and me.

"Because of the fond feelings I have about all of you, I'm not going to turn these four in for the punishment they certainly

....

10 The beginning of the *rubedo* stage.

deserve. But they can't just go on as if nothing had happened, so I've decided that they alone will be excluded from the seventh and culminating action, more glorious than all the rest. That's punishment enough, and in this way they won't incur any further blame from Their Majesties."

Well you can imagine how we felt on hearing this. The young mistress certainly knew how to look stern, and we were soon crying our eyes out and believing we had just the worst possible luck. The young mistress sent one of the many handmaids that were always standing around to fetch the musicians, who were to blast us out the door with cornets, and they were so full of scorn and derision they could hardly blow for laughing. What hurt more was that our mistress laughed so hard at our grief, anger and distress; and it seemed that even some of our former companions weren't all that upset about our disgrace.

The reality was actually very different. As soon as we went out and shut the door behind us, the musicians whispered to us to be brave and follow them up a winding stair. This led to a chamber *above* the seventh level,[11] right under the roof – and there was the old warder of the tower, whom we hadn't seen all day, standing atop a small round furnace. He greeted us warmly and congratulated us that we'd been chosen for the final tasks by our young mistress. When we explained what *we*

....

11 This most important of all the chambers in the seven-towered castle is the *eighth* – which to my mind gives a bit more support to the idea that *CW* is best understood as a tale in eight days.

thought had happened, he laughed till his belly shook, that we had thought our good luck was so bad.

"It goes to show, dear boys," he said, "that men never know what good God means to do them."

While we were talking, the young mistress came running in with her box of bird-ashes, and (after she'd finished laughing at us) she emptied the ashes into a different container and filled her own box with other stuff. "I've got to go now and pull some wool over the other workers' eyes," she said. "You stay here and do whatever the warder tells you to do. And work hard—just as you really did work before."

She went down onto the seventh level, opened the opening, and called down to our companions on the sixth to come up. What she did with them, or told them to do, I can't say, for they were strictly forbidden to speak of it after, and we were too busy to spy on them. What we up above did was to saturate the bird's ashes with the prepared waters until they became a thin paste. Then we cooked the paste in the furnace, and when it was hot we poured it into two little molds and set them to cool. We had some time then to peek down at our fellows below through a couple of openings in the floor. They were very busy at a furnace of their own, blowing on the fire with a pipe. They stood around, taking turns blowing madly, thinking they were the important ones and doing the important stuff. Then our old tutor called us to work again, and I don't know what happened down there.

We opened our little molds – and inside were two beautiful,

bright, nearly transparent figures, a male and a female, each about four inches long. They were like nothing I'd ever seen, and perhaps like nothing anybody has ever seen. They weren't hard, but flexible and fleshly, like actual human bodies, though they were lifeless. I was immediately reminded of the body of Lady Venus that I had seen; I'm sure it was made similarly.

We laid these angelic babes on two little satin cushions, and for a long time we just stared at them, too stunned by their delicate beauty to do anything. The old warder wanted us to get busy and feed them with the blood of the dead bird (which had been saved in a golden cup). We were to do this by dripping it drop by drop into their tiny mouths. It made them grow, definitely, and as they grew they became proportionately more beautiful than when they were small. If the best painters of the world could have been shown them, they'd have seen how far Nature can outstrip anything they can do! Finally they were so big that we had to lift them from the cushions and lay them on a long table covered with fine white velvet. The old warder told us to cover them up to the breast with double silk taffeta, which we almost didn't want to do, they were so unspeakably lovely. We had used up nearly all the bird blood on them, and they were perfect and fully grown; they had long, golden-yellow hair. That body of Venus that I saw had nothing on them.

They had as yet no warmth, no senses. They were dead statues, though they looked so natural and lifelike. The old warder made it clear we had to be careful not to let them grow too big, so he told us to stop the feeding and covered their faces as well with the

by Christian Rosencreutz 175

...I could make out a small opening, now shut —
none of the others noticed it.

silk. Bright torches were then set all around the table. I have to say that there was no real reason for the torches – the old warder had ordered them put there only so that we couldn't see the souls that were soon going to enter into these bodies. I myself wouldn't have been on the lookout for this big event if I hadn't seen those flames of spirit twice before. I said nothing about that to my fellows and didn't let the old warder know what I knew, either.

He asked us to sit on a bench opposite the table. After a time our mistress came in, with musicians and other accouterments, including two exquisite white garments such as I had not seen anywhere in the castle. I can't describe them; they seemed somehow made of crystal, but they were soft, and not transparent – well, I just don't know what more to say. She laid them on a table, and when she had seated her maidens around the room she and the old warder began a series of actions intended to seem magical but which were only to distract us from what was actually happening.[12] Remember, we were in the chamber just below the roof, which was curiously shaped: it arched upward in seven concave hemispheres, six around a central one, in which I could make out a small opening, now shut – none of the others noticed it.

After enough of this legerdemain, six maidens entered the chamber, each carrying a long funnel around which was

....

12 This secrecy and misdirection has roots in the alchemists' elaborate ruses to keep others from understanding their processes. Those who know, know – as Christian does here.

wrapped a wreath of green, glittering, flammable material. The old warder took one of these, and after he had removed a couple of the torches at the head of the table, he placed one of the funnels in the mouth of the male body so that the wide end was directly under that opening in the roof. My companions were staring at the figures on the table, but I knew better – as soon as the papery wreath around the funnel was set afire, I saw the hole open above and a bright stream of fire shoot down the tube into the body. The opening in the roof immediately closed, and the old warder removed the funnel. The figure then definitely began to blink his eyes, though he barely moved otherwise, and my fellows of course thought that it had been the burning wreath of stuff that had brought him to life. Another funnel was then placed in his mouth, and the stuff around it lit, and the opening opened, and more soul went down through the tube.

The whole process was gone through three times for each figure; then all the torches were put out and carried away. The white velvet covering of the table was folded over the faintly stirring bodies. A farther room was then unlocked, to reveal a nuptial or birthing bed, which had been prepared for them. We carried the couple to the bedchamber, the velvet wrappings were taken off them, and they were put gently to bed close together. We drew the bed-curtains around them and left them there to sleep a long while.

The young mistress went off meantime to see how her other workers were doing. She later told me that they were very happy, because they were at the work of making gold – which is certainly a part of the Great Art, though not the main part, or the best, or the most valuable. They'd been given a portion of the dead bird's ashes, so they believed that this was what the whole process had been for, and the gold they produced would be the thing that brought life to the dead.

But we all the while sat very still, waiting for the married couple to wake up. We'd only been waiting half an hour or so when who should fly into the chamber but little Cupid![13] After he'd greeted us all in his merry way, he flew to the bed, pulled open the curtains, and began teasing and pestering the couple there until they woke up! They were completely amazed to find themselves where they were, because as far as they knew[14] they'd simply lain asleep from the moment they'd lost their heads till now. Cupid introduced them to each other, then stepped aside so that they could recover a little. Meantime he kept up his old tricks with the rest of us. "We need some music in here! I want music to cheer up these long faces!" So we had to go call in those musicians, who struck up a tune.

In a while our mistress returned. She humbly greeted the king

....

13 We shouldn't be surprised to see him here, since he is associated with his mother, Venus, whom Christian discovered in the same beautiful translucent inanimate state.

14 I find it wonderful and touching that in *CW* the participants in the allegory of the alchemical process seem such real persons. The royal couple apparently had no idea that this was going to be the outcome of their beheading.

and queen (who were still feeling a little faint) and kissed their hands. She brought them those two strange garments I tried to describe before and helped them on with them; then they stepped forth. Two fine but very odd throne-chairs were put out for them, and there they sat. We all congratulated them with the greatest reverence, and the king whispered how grateful he was to all of us, and that we were all in his very good graces.

It was five o'clock now, and the king and queen had to depart as soon as all their important regalia could be loaded onto the ships. We accompanied the royal couple all the way down the winding stairs, through all the doors and the surrounding walls and battlements, down to their ship in the harbor. They got on board, with a number of maidens and Cupid, and sailed away so swiftly that they were soon out of sight. I learned later that several tall ships came out to meet them, and in just four hours they'd crossed those many leagues of sea.

The musicians now had to carry all of our things from the tower into the other ships and make them ready for the return journey. This was taking a very long time, so the old warder gave an order, and a number of soldiers appeared who had been concealed in alcoves in the thickness of the wall. (I realized then that the tower was well protected against attack.) These soldiers made quick work of the packing and loading of our stuff, so there was nothing more for us to do but go have some supper.

When the table was all laid, the young mistress brought the four of us who'd been called the "lazy sluggards" in among our companions again. We were supposed to behave as though we were very downcast and all, and not laugh.[15] Those others grinned smugly at one another, though it seemed a few of them did feel a little sorry for us as well. The old warder had supper with us, and he was a sharp moderator of our table talk: no one could give a clever opinion that he couldn't turn right around, or stand on its head, and improve on – or at least speak knowledgeably about. I learned a good deal from that gentleman. It would be a fine thing if everyone could go and sit at his feet, and study his methods. Things wouldn't go wrong so often and so disastrously in the world.

After supper, he took us into his cabinets of curiosities, which were built here and there in the bulwarks of the tower, and we saw so many astonishing natural products, and so many equally astonishing products of human invention in imitation of Nature,[16] that we could have spent a year there studying them.

....

15 Why the brotherhood should be built on tricks that separate some of the brothers from others is not explained – it's just so.

16 Lorraine Daston and Katherine Park in their book *Wonders and the Order of Nature* (Zone Books, 1998) show how the Renaissance and Baroque imagination saw human works of art and craft as in competition with the productions of Nature (jewels, wonders, monsters, treasures), as though Nature were basically a superb artist. Early museums and collections were full of natural oddities next to works of art, and natural objects made more wonderful by being worked on by human artists – bejeweled, or inscribed, or embellished.

We went over them by lamplight long into the night, but at last all we wanted to study was our beds; so we were taken to rooms cut in the wall of the tower, where the beds were rich and fine, and so were all the furnishings, which made us wonder why we'd had to make do with such skimpy accommodations before. From eleven o'clock at night till eight the next morning I slept soundly there, relieved now of all work and worry, tired after all the labors of the day and hearing the gentle hushing of the sea.

The Seventh Day

I woke up past eight and got ready quickly so that I could return to the tower, but the many dark passages in the wall led in so many directions that I wandered around for quite a while before I found the way out. The same thing happened to the others, until we finally gathered in the bottom chamber of the tower that had been our laboratory. There our lady had a new robe for each of us, all of yellow, and our Golden Fleece decorations were returned to us. When this was done, she told us at last the secret name of our order: we were all *Knights of the Golden Stone.*

After breakfast, the old warder presented us each with a gold medallion. On one side of it were these letters: AR. NAT. MI, which stood for *"Ars, Naturae Ministra,"* or "Art, the Servant of Nature." On the other face it had TEM. NA. F., standing for *"Temporis natura filia,"* or "Nature, the Daughter of Time." He warned us strictly[1] not to try to take anything else with us from the tower.

We went down to the harbor, where our ships lay, but now far

....

[1] It's likely that the processes employed in the Olympus Tower are useless or even harmful anywhere else, though ambitious alchemical workers like these might be tempted to try them out.

more richly decorated than before – it was impossible that all these amazing furnishings hadn't been brought over in advance. There were now twelve ships, our remaining six and six of the old warder's, which he had manned with well-armed soldiers. He himself, though, joined all of us knights in the flagship. Before us went a ship filled with musicians (he employed any number of musicians, apparently) to entertain us. Our banners were the twelve signs of the Zodiac, and the banner of our ship was Libra; it had a wonderful clock on deck, among other things, that showed not only hours but minutes.[2] The sea was so calm that it was delightful to be on it, but the best thing of all was the old warder's conversation. He knew so many wonderful stories I could have spent a lifetime listening to him.

We must have been traveling fast, for before we'd been at sea two hours, the lookout called out that he could now see the bay beyond, almost covered in ships – it seemed they must be on their way out to meet us, and in fact as soon as we had come through the channel into the bay, there were *five hundred* ships over the water! One grand one glittered with gold and gems, and the king and queen sat there with many lords and ladies and high-born maidens. As soon as we came in sight, their ship fired its cannon, and there was such a blast of trumpets,

....

2 Clocks that showed minutes were still rare in Andreae's day. Around the time that *CW* was written, the great clockmaker-mathematician Jost Burgi is said to have invented (and made an instrument that could count by) seconds.

trombones, and kettledrums that all the ships seemed to dance on the water. The sailors brought our ships together, and there we dropped anchor. Old Atlas, the royal astronomer, stepped out from beside the royal couple and made a brief but elegant speech, offering us the king's welcome and asking if we had brought him the Royal Gift.

Now imagine how confused and astounded most of our brother knights were as to how this king and queen could have got here – they expected they would now have to awaken those corpses buried in the garden! We four who knew better didn't enlighten them, and pretended to be just as surprised as they were. The old warder then came forward and answered Atlas's speech with a somewhat longer reply, in which he wished the king and queen all happiness and many children, etc., after which he brought out a very curious little casket.[3] I don't know at all what was in it. The old warder gave it to Cupid – who had been hovering between the king and the queen – for him to keep.

Another celebratory volley from the cannons, and on we sailed, till we arrived at a different port than the one we'd first

....

3 Montgomery thinks that the mysterious gift must be the crucifix formed from a single pearl that Christian observed being carried between the couple on their way to the play and the execution. Since he believes that the rebirth and reuniting of the king and queen are an allegory of the marriage of Christ and the Church, the connection seems obvious to him.

by Christian Rosencreutz 187

set out from – this one was near the gate at which I had first gone into the castle. There was a huge crowd awaiting us there, many of the king's household, and hundreds of horses. As we went ashore, the king and queen both gave us their hands, every one of us, with great kindness.

So we were to mount up and ride the rest of the way to the castle entrance. Now here I have to ask you not to take what I have to tell as pride or boasting on my part – believe me that I wouldn't even bother to tell the next incident, probably, if I didn't have to. What happened was that all our company from the island was mixed with the lords and ladies from the castle, but the old warder and I (myself completely undeserving) were alone invited to ride beside the king and were each given a snow-white banner with a red cross to bear. Very likely I was only chosen because of my age, he and I being the only graybeards there.

I'd fastened to my hat (where once my four roses had been) those two tokens that the gatekeepers had given me when I first came to enter the castle. The young king took an interest in them.

"So you were the one who was able to buy these tokens at the gate?" he asked me.

I bowed and murmured very humbly, "Yes."

The king laughed and said, "No need any longer for little tokens! You are, after all, *my father!*"[4]

....

4 This apparently simple statement has given much trouble to

Then he asked me what I had paid for the tokens with.

"One with water and one with salt," I answered.

"Well!" he answered. "And how did you come to make such wise choices?"

I grew a little more confident at that and told him what had happened with my bread, and the dove, and the raven, and all that, and he was very pleased with the story. "It shows that God intended you to succeed here," he said.

Just then we came to the first gate. The porter in the blue coat waited there, holding a petition, and as soon as he saw me beside the king, he gave this petition to me, begging me to remind the king how generously he, the porter, had treated me.

I asked the king about this man, what sort of person he was.

"He was once a very famous and celebrated astrologer," the king said readily. "My father the king held him in high regard. Once upon a time, though, he committed a grave error: he snuck in to spy on the goddess Venus asleep in her bed. Of course he was found out and punished, and his punishment

....

interpreters. Rudolf Steiner (founder of Anthroposophy) takes it to mean that Christian is the father of his own "transformed faculties of knowledge" symbolized by the King. Jung sees it as a little metafictional joke: Christian, thus Andreae, is the "father" of *all* the characters in his book, a fact that a character in the book is here reminding him of. Much as I like that idea, I think a simpler interpretation is preferable: that the King recognizes Christian as the father, or one of the fathers, of his reborn self, thus needing no tokens to be in his presence.

was this: he must wait at this first gate until someone comes along who can release him."

"How," I asked, "can he be released?"

"If someone can be discovered to have committed the same fault as he," the king replied, "then that person must take the porter's place, and the porter will be freed."

This went like a shot right to my heart, for of course I was myself that guilty person. I said nothing, though, and only gave the porter's petition to the king. When he had read it, he seemed quite alarmed – the queen, who with the Duchess of the Weights rode right behind him, noticed it. "What is it, my lord?" she asked. "What does the letter say?"

But the king brushed it off, put away the letter, and began to talk of other things, until about three o'clock we arrived at the castle and accompanied the king as he went into his hall.

The king immediately called for old Atlas his astronomer and with him retreated to a private room where (as I would learn) he showed Atlas the porter's petition and ordered Atlas to ride immediately to the porter to find out more.

The king then joined us, and with his spouse took his seat amid the other lords and ladies.

Our young mistress spoke up, praising us all for our hard work and all the effort and sacrifice we had made. She asked that we all be royally rewarded, and asked that she too might receive what was due to her for fulfilling her commission. At that the old warder rose and testified to everything our mistress had said, and agreed that both she and we should be well compensated. What the king decided was that we were each to step up and make a wish of any kind, and it would be granted – because surely men of good minds such as ourselves would make wise wishes. We had until after supper to think about what our wish would be.

To pass the time till supper, the king and queen began playing a board game somewhat like chess, except that it had different rules, because it was played with Virtues against Vices – it was very ingenious the traps that a Vice could set for a Virtue, and the ways that a Virtue could escape and trap a Vice. It was so well-thought-out and took such cleverness to play that I wish we had the same game.

During the game, old Atlas came in again and whispered in the king's ear. I sat and blushed – my guilty conscience was pricking me. The king summoned me and gave me the petition to read for myself, and it was about just what I guessed it would be about. The porter began by wishing the king prosperity and wealth and that his offspring might flourish far and wide and so on. Then he claimed that the time was come at last when he ought to be released from his servitude, *because he had learned that Venus had been uncovered and looked at by one of the king's guests.* He had irrefutable evidence of this, he said, and if His Majesty would make the same investigation, he would find that in fact it was true, she had been intruded upon; and if this turned out to be *not* so, then he, the porter, was willing to stand at his gate for the rest of his life. Lastly he begged that he, even at the risk of his life and his happiness, might be allowed to come to this night's supper in order to help identify the offender, and thus win his own freedom.

All this was powerfully expressed and showed the noble nature of the man, but to me it cut like a knife, and I wished I'd never had to see it. I thought desperately of some way to use my royal wish to resolve this, and I asked the king if there wasn't something else that could be done so that the porter could be freed without leaving his post and disrupting the party with all this scandal.

"Oh no," the king said. "Because of the special nature of his case, there's only one way out for him. For this one night, we can let him come here as he asks."

So someone was sent to bring him in.

Supper was laid in a spacious refectory which we'd never been in before, which was so perfect – but I'm at a loss how to describe it. We were conducted in with all pomp and circumstance. Cupid, however, was absent: he was, I was told, rather angry about the insult to his sleeping mother. In fact, the offense, which was actually my own, and the porter's petition revealing it, made for a lot of disquiet: the king was doubtful how to go about making inquiries among the guests, because asking would reveal what none of them – all but one – so far knew. So he allowed the porter – who by then had arrived and been admitted – to see what he could learn, examining each of us, while the king himself tried to make the dinner as cheerful and convivial as he could.

Eventually everyone did liven up, and a brilliant conversation ensued, with all kinds of entertaining and perspicuous remarks and anecdotes. I can't bring myself to describe how all the ceremonies and so forth that followed were carried out; it's not necessary to the story I am trying to tell, and it's not the reader's business, but I'll say that it wasn't just the amounts we drank that made the talk seem wise and the ceremonies profound – no, this was the noblest, as it was the last, meal at which I was present. When it was all done, the tables were whisked away and a number of highly wrought chairs were set out in a circle, and all of us sat, including the king, the queen, their aged counselors Atlas and the old warder, and all the ladies and maidens.

A handsome young page then opened that beautiful little black book, and Atlas took the center of the circle and spoke. He said that His Royal Majesty hadn't forgotten the services we had rendered, and how carefully we had done our duty, and for that reason he had elected us all Knights of the Golden Stone.[5] He asked us to serve him further if ever he needed us, and also to swear to a number of principles. If we did so, His Majesty would treat us, his followers, well.

Atlas turned the page then and read the articles:

You knights shall swear that you will not give credit for our

....

5 Specifically not Knights of the Red Cross or Rosicrucian Brothers. They were formerly Knights of the Golden Fleece – on a quest, like Jason. Now they are Knights of the achieved Philosopher's Stone.

by Christian Rosencreutz 193

Order and its works to any demon or spirit but only to God,
your Creator, and to Nature, his handmaid.

That you will hate all immorality and excess and whoring,
and not dirty your Order with such things.

That you will help any worthy person that you can with your
skills.

That you will not use this honor for worldly profit or power.

That you won't go on living longer than God wants you to.

We had to laugh at that last article; maybe it was put in after
the others just for a joke.[6]

We swore to all of this on the king's scepter and thereupon
were installed as knights with all the usual ceremonies. Among
the privileges granted us was power to work effectively in our
own judgment against Ignorance, Poverty, and Illness. We were
brought all together to a little chapel, and our knighthoods
were ratified there, and thanks given to God. Everyone had to
write his name in that chapel, and this is what I wrote:

The highest knowledge is to know you know nothing.[7]

....

6 Immortality was a goal of alchemy – the Philosopher's Stone was
also the Elixir of Life. These Knights are foreswearing such a personal
pursuit – their skills are to be used to help others.

7 A variant of the remark of Socrates – "I know only one thing, that I
know nothing." It also seems to reflect Christian's dejection at having
passed so many tests and yet failed in the end.

Brother Christian Rosencreutz
Knight of the Golden Stone
A.D. *1459*

Everyone else wrote what they thought was appropriate, and we returned to the hall, where it was time to come up with that wish that we'd been promised would be granted. The king and his council went off into a smaller chamber to hear what we wanted, one at a time. Since each of us went in alone, I don't know what the others wished for. For myself, I thought that the most laudable thing I could do was to demonstrate some particular virtue in my wish, in honor of my Order; and I believe the most honorable virtue, anyway the one that's always cost me the most to exercise, is Gratitude. Of course I could have wished for something precious and gratifying to myself, but I managed to suppress that impulse and vowed that I'd try to free the porter, my benefactor, even if it cost me everything.

So now I was called in. First the king asked me if, after I read the porter's petition, I'd been able to glean anything about that reprobate among us. I didn't hesitate; I just started in as plainly as I could to tell the whole story of how it was I myself who had stupidly fallen into that error, and I offered to take the punishment I deserved. The king and his council were dumbfounded at this sudden outburst and asked me to step outside for a moment.

I waited in agony while they debated, and when I was called in again, it was old Atlas who spoke to me.

Well, the answer was that my wish couldn't be used to wish that.

❧

"The king is so sorry that you, Brother, you of all people, one he loved above all the rest, stumbled so. But he just can't go against our ancient customs. The old porter must be freed – and *you* must take his place." He said the king hoped that eventually someone else who did what I had done might be discovered and apprehended, but the soonest that could happen would be at the wedding of his own son.[8]

This judgment almost killed me. I hated myself and my babbling tongue – why couldn't I have just shut up! – but I soon got hold of myself.[9] I told the king and his lords how this

....

8 An unexpected and yet winning aspect of this story to me is that the death and resurrection of the king (and queen) really have very little effect either on them or on the world. They've returned more beautiful and perhaps more noble (there's no knowing), but they are essentially the same. The true and final aim of the alchemical Work – the creation of the Philosopher's Stone from the copulation of the Red King and the White Woman – doesn't happen, at least within the compass of the tale, and here the king predicts that his own son will have to undergo the same process he did, and will therefore be flawed and mortal like himself. (It may be that the old king and his spouse who were beheaded were in actual fact the young king's parents).

9 It may be – Montgomery is certain of it – that the labors and the visions that Christian has undergone have made it possible for him to do this selfless deed. All the other redemptions (of the emperor in the weights trial, of the king and queen) cost him nothing of himself – but this one does. It is a key concept in Christianity as in alchemy

porter had given me a token, and had also sent a note recommending me to the next porter, and by their help I had got into the castle and stood up to the trial of the weights, and because of that I had been able to be part of all the wonders and delights that followed.

"Now it's only fair that I should show gratitude to my benefactor," I said, "because without him none of that would have happened. So thank you, my lords, for your sentence. I'm willing and ready to accept some burden for his sake.

"But now there is, if you please, the matter of my own wish for myself. And my wish, if it can be granted – it's to be back in my home under the hill again."

You see, my idea was that I could free the porter by my confession, and then my own wish could free me. Well, the answer was that my wish couldn't be used to wish that. My wish that the porter go free, though, was granted, and the king said he was very pleased I had acted so generously, even though he was afraid I still didn't know how bad a fix I had got myself into through my curiosity.

Anyway that good man was pronounced free, and I was sent out.

After me, others went in and came back out again happy as could be, which stung me all over again, since it seemed

....

that the seeker must expend all of himself to find that by which he will be restored to himself – he can't save himself, but must trust in the powers he solicits.

by Christian Rosencreutz 199

certain that I would live out my life sitting by that gate. Many gloomy thoughts were running around in my head, about what I was going to do, and how I would pass the time; and my final thought was that since I'm old and very likely haven't much longer to live, this anguish and my humiliating job would quickly finish me off, and then my door-keeping would be over, and I could sleep in my grave. On the one hand it bothered me terribly that I had seen such superb things, only to be robbed of them. On the other I was glad that at least I had been accepted and found worthy, and not forced to depart in shame.

While I was brooding, the rest of the knights had got ready, and after the king and his lords had said good night to each one, they were taken to their rooms. But I, wretched man, had nobody to show me where I was to go, and all I could do was stand there tormenting myself. And just so that I would never forget for a moment my lowly function, I was made to put on the iron ring that the old porter had worn.

Finally the king spoke to me.

"This is the last time you are likely to see me as my guest and companion," he said, "but remember that still you should always behave as a knight, and follow the rules of the Order you have sworn to." He took me in his arms and kissed me, and by all this I knew for certain that in the morning I must in fact sit at my gate.

The other knights stayed to say a few kind words to me, and gave me their hands at last, asking God to protect me, and so on. Then the two old men, Atlas and the old warder, took me into a fine bedchamber, where there were three beds. Each of us took one, and there we spent almost two[...]

Here two pages or so are missing. The author of the foregoing, though he supposed that in the morning he would have to become the porter of the castle, in fact returned home.

[THE EIGHTH DAY]

Here two pages or so are missing. The author of the foregoing, though he supposed that in the morning he would have to become the porter of the castle, in fact returned home.

This is the strangest turn this strange tale makes. Some commentaries, perhaps baffled, don't even mention it. It is in one sense a further metafictional swerve – a new omniscient narrative frame is suddenly introduced, calling into question the provenance of the whole story. But how does this new voice come to know what happened to Christian? It might be thought that Andreae got tired of his story and simply drew this line across it. But if so, why not end with "In the end he was allowed to return home" (i.e., because another sinner was found to take his place)? No, he goes home *the next morning* – on the eighth day of this romance – without explanation. It could have perhaps ended with "In the morning the king sent word that Christian's wish was granted and he could go home after all" – but no, that's not even hinted at. I have wondered if Christian simply refused the task – like Alice in the trial at the end of *Alice in Wonderland* discovering that her tormentors are all nothing but a pack of cards. He forgave himself, and walked away. That would assort ill with the generous and moving resolve he showed, and the seriousness with which he took his sin and his expiation. It might be that Andreae is simply wrapping up his shaggy-dog story and letting us see it was all a joke. I don't know. I don't believe it's an error; I think it has meaning. I just don't know what it is.

Andres Paniagua, who checked my translation and notes against the original German editions, wonders if Andreae could be suggesting that the story is actually cyclic: perhaps Christian exists within a story loop, where he actually gets to redeem himself, so that the story can return to its beginning and start again. That would be consistent with his being recognized on several occasions as someone who has been expected, and also with the indications I have pointed out that the royal redemption process happens over and over. I think this is a delightful notion, and though it seems to be one impossible for Andreae in the seventeenth century to have had, at least consciously, that needn't stop us from entertaining it. In a famous essay, Jorge Luis Borges suggested that the very existence of Kafka in the twentieth century creates the "Kafkaesque" qualities of writers who preceded him. It can be posited that the current existence of metafictional science fiction (particularly if I'm right that *CW* is a science fiction novel a*vant la lettre*) can in a real sense bring into being the post-modernist time-loop qualities of a tale told long ago. That is the strange alchemy of story.

JOHN CROWLEY is a writer of fictions of various kinds. He was born in the appropriately liminal town of Presque Isle, Maine, and from there journeyed to different places. He lives now in Massachusetts west of the Connecticut River and works part time teaching at Yale University. Insofar as it is his, and depending on how they are counted, this is his sixteenth published book.

Since illustrating *The Chemical Wedding* THEO FADEL has discovered she is the eleventh great grandniece of Robert Fludd who defended the Rosy Cross manuscripts in 1616. He mentions building his own wooden robots and *other things* impossible by "mere mathematics without the co-operation of natural magic."*

Theo lives in Holyoke, Massachusetts with her spouse Ruth and four cats in a charmingly old house that stands by natural magic. A native Charlottean and enthusiastic somnambulist, she grew up within a half mile of PTL's broadcast studio and Billy Graham's mother, watching *Star Trek* and *Batman* in a Peter Max bathrobe. When science sacrificed the moon program she turned to *Dungeons & Dragons*. She has a BA in Archeology from Bryn Mawr College and a Master of Architecture from Columbia University. She studied drawing, sculpture and painting at the Art Students League, NYC while working in an old German cabinet shop. Her first day there an aged Austrian said "One hundred years and you're the first woman we've seen." Currently her studio is in Easthampton, her website is theofadel.com and she's been in Massachusetts less than a hundred years. This is the first book she has illustrated.

....

* Craven, J. (1902). *Doctor Robert Fludd (Robertus de Fluctibus), the English Rosicrucian : Life and writings.* (p. 44). Kirkwall: W. Peace.

by Christian Rosencreutz 209

Printed in the USA
CPSIA information can be obtained
at www.ICGtesting.com
JSHW011156251023
50846JS00001B/1